RAGGED

"*Ragged* boldly stakes a claim on literary territory previously mapped by Kenneth Grahame, then rewrites the map with a sophisticated literary cartography that is entirely modern, and entirely Christopher Irvin's own. It is the work of a novelist entirely in charge of his material, and one with talent to burn. A delightful and original novel."—MICHAEL ROWE, author of *Enter, Night* and *Wild Fell*

"An imaginative spin on the crime fiction genre."—*THE NEW YORK TIMES*

"Irvin's tone is lightning fast, hard-hitting, and leaves the reader breathless and shocked with the sudden and realistic portrayal of violence."—LITREACTOR

RAGGED

CHRISTOPHER IRVIN

TITAN BOOKS

RAGGED

Print edition ISBN: 9781789097863
E-book edition ISBN: 9781789097870

Published by Titan Books
A division of Titan Publishing Group Ltd
144 Southwark Street, London SE1 0UP
www.titanbooks.com

First Titan edition: April 2022
10 9 8 7 6 5 4 3 2 1

This is a work of fiction. All of the characters, organizations, and events portrayed in this novel are either products of the author's imagination or are used fictitiously. Any resemblance to actual persons, living or dead (except for satirical purposes), is entirely coincidental.

A CIP catalogue record for this title is available from the British Library.

Printed and bound by CPI Group (UK) Ltd, Croydon, CR0 4YY

For George and Frederick

LIKE AUTUMN LEAVES FALL HER TEARS

In the heart of the Woods, Winifred leaned against an ancient maple and pressed a damp kerchief against her eyes, her skin raw from tears shed along the walk. It was late fall and yet the tree clung to most of its leaves, their beautiful reddish-purple hue visible in the pale moonlight. The beauty provided a false sense of hope, an image of permanence that it might last the winter. One by one the leaves would fall as the cold crept along the tree's limbs. And so too would she.

The breeze picked up, plucking a large leaf from the maple and flinging it against Winifred. She brought her wounded arm up and pressed the leaf against her chest. She felt the infection spreading from the bite with each pulse of her heart, corrupting her blood and tickling her brain.

A hint of wood smoke drifting through the night air tingled Winifred's nose as she left the tree and approached the nearby General Store. She'd dressed in layers, overly warm for the trek, yet still felt the night's chill press through her fur. She paused, still clutching the leaf, and took a deep breath to compose herself—which only brought on more tears. The strongest recollections are intertwined with smell, and for Winifred, a dog with a very active nose, each sniff brought a burst of memories, all of which tore at her, and despite being so dear to her heart, felt so far away. Lazy summer strolls with her strong and wonderful mutt of a husband. Watching her two pups grow into their own, too fast. Looking back, there was never a dull moment, never enough time. Winifred dabbed her eyes once more, pocketed the kerchief and willed herself forward into the shop.

The miniature bell above the door remained quiet as Winifred stepped across the threshold. The sparse shelves were dotted with fat, greasy candles that gave off a warm glow undeserving of the near-empty shop. Cal had warned her that the caravan was late with supplies, but she had to get out of the house, had to see for herself. She ran a paw along the nearest barren shelf, her pads coming up thick with dust.

"Winifred!" Duchess, a hedgehog, owner and proprietor of the General Store, looked up from her workspace on the counter at the back of the shop, a wide smile across her face. She removed her apron as she rounded the counter and walked as fast as her short legs would carry her, headed for Winifred, arms wide and welcoming.

"My darling, what brings you in at such a late hour? I was just closing up, but of course I'll remain open for as long as you need, old friend. I'm afraid I've not much to offer, other than conversation, which I hope suits you as it has been much too long and—"

Duchess stopped mid-sentence as she reached Winifred. She leaned in and sniffed the air beneath Winifred's chin, around her wounded arm that still clutched the maple leaf. Duchess wrinkled her nose and took a step back, concerned, her embrace withdrawn. "You're not well."

Winifred took Duchess's paw, gave it a long, soft squeeze and looked her in the eye. "A stiff cold is all. I wanted to see you. Thought you might have some medicine on hand."

"Oh dear, oh dear." Duchess eyed the ground, contemplating the matter, then looked past Winifred, through the door, out at the darkness surrounding them. "Come. Come have a seat in the back. I'll blow out some of these candles and join you in a moment. I've no medicine, but I'll pour us some strong tea. I've been heating a kettle to wash up and head home, but what's good for a wash is good for a drink. I promise to leaf out the soap. That's worth at least a little chuckle, no?"

Winifred cracked the smallest of smiles. "Thank you."

"We're right on our way to feeling better." Duchess returned the light squeeze and tended the candles while Winifred made her way toward the back. The store was in a sad state. Aside from a few bags of flour lurking along the bottom shelves, it lacked the most basic dry goods. Unlabeled cans were scattered here and there among cooking utensils, a burlap sack with a hole spilling dried beans, and a few other lumps she couldn't quite make out in the shadows. There was a time when many traders passed through the Woods. They hawked their goods door-to-door willy-nilly whenever they felt like it. The Two Old Cats caravan, *Professional and Prompt*, had outlasted them all. Their large wagon stuffed the General Store with all manner of goods and wares several times a year. Now that the Two Old Cats were, indeed, literally quite old, there was worry of when their business would end, and who might take over. Duchess had told Winifred in the past that it would be rude to inquire about the two cat sisters (or their trusted moose) about when they might hang up their straps, and so she let it be. Winifred wasn't the only one wishing someone had gone out on a limb and asked anyway. Late was one thing; never to return, quite another.

Duchess pulled a wooden spoon from a rack and gave it a tap against her paw. "Not a pretty sight, is it? How do you think I feel, staring at the shelves all day, turning away disappointed customers? Those damn cats will be the death of us. You'd think they could pick a summer month to be late. No, of course not. I've half a mind to go out and start looking for them myself."

"I'll happily join you."

"Not looking like that you won't." The hedgehog pulled two mugs from beneath the counter. She set them before Winifred and disappeared into a back room. Winifred dabbed a paw against her damp forehead. She wondered if she looked worse than when she'd left the house, but there was no mirror in the shop to confirm. The rag knotted around her wrist concealing the wound was still tight. She'd hid the bite from Cal at first, but soon after she arrived home the fever struck and he quickly saw through her white lies. However, she stuck to her story that she'd been bitten on the Woods' side of the river, even though she knew Cal didn't believe her. She'd always been good at small fibs, but when it came to serious matters, anxiety got the best of her when put on the spot.

A moment later Duchess returned with a hot kettle in one paw, a cluster of dried tea leaves in the other.

"Watch yourself, now." Duchess crumbled the leaves over the two mugs (and the counter between) and filled them with hot water.

"Drink up. The longer it lingers, the more bitter it gets." Duchess took a deep pull. "Like my customers!" she added, making herself chuckle.

Winifred gritted her teeth as she tasted the earthy liquid, closed her eyes as the pain in her arm flared. She never should have gone back into the Fells. Should have told the damn rabbit to go himself, or told the old bear to send another one of his pawns. She'd done enough over the years for him in penance for Cal, hadn't she? Her agreement to become one of the bear's informants—his eyes and ears who kept tabs on the landscape surrounding his mount—had kept him off her husband's back once Cal left his old life in the Fells behind. She'd been able to maintain her role in secret . . . *and look where that led you*, she thought, feeling a twinge of the usual pang of guilt at hiding something so serious from her husband. Hell, Old Brown should have come down from his mount himself if he was so worried about the spread of infection. *And here I am*, she thought, *bringing it home*. Worse, she didn't even get a good look at the creature that had bitten her, all covered with mud and debris as it was. Too concerned with running from the scent of a nearby posse of vermin out on patrol from the Rubbish Heap to do her job.

"It tastes . . . good," Winifred said, lowering her mug.

"Don't lie. It tastes like dirt, ha! Always made me feel good, though. Even when Mother made me choke it down as a youngster. What a brat I was."

After a quiet moment, Duchess asked, "How is Cal?"

Winifred forced down another gulp of tea, lit up as she thought of her family. "He's wonderful. Same with the pups. A pair of wild animals, rarely able to sit still."

"Just like their father, though staying out of trouble, I hope."

Winifred took another sip of her tea, nodded. "All three of them."

"I fondly recall those late nights selling food to Cal out of the back of my store. This was before you arrived in town. We were all much younger—especially Cal—and the community found it hard to trust a dog who spent so much time outside of the Woods."

"Cal's told me on several occasions how much he appreciated your kindness."

"He was a good sport. My mother always said, 'a customer is a customer.' We welcome all and do our best to remain neutral when it comes to rumor and politics.

"I told him he could have come to the front like all the other customers, but he worried about hurting my business—as if they had any place else to go!"

Winifred leaned against the counter in an attempt to hide her discomfort, her legs suddenly weak. The fever had returned, coming on strong, worse than before.

"I'm afraid I must return home and get some rest. Thank you very much for the company and tea."

"Please take care of yourself. I hope to see more of you. Finish your tea on the way home, and tell that husband of yours you must do the shopping when the caravan arrives in order to return the cup."

"You're a wonderful friend, Duchess."

Winfred shivered, her entire body trembling as she wandered toward home. She kept her eyes on the ground, focused on each step as her memories of the night began to fade, her mind shrouded in the darkness of the night.

PART 1

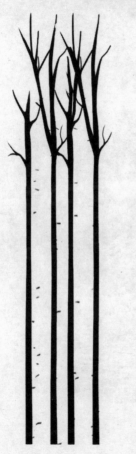

THE

RIVER

BANK

1

Cal sat along the riverbank atop a wind-swept pile of dry, dead leaves. Bare feet at the water's edge, pea coat buttoned to his chin. The ancestry of his mixed breed had been lost to time, but if you'd been fortunate to be in the company of a variety of the *Canis lupus familiaris*, you might think his facial features resembled that of a beagle: dusty white from nose to top of skull blending with a reddish-brown along the sides of his face and lower jaw, eyes sharp with a tinge of sadness, and long ears that dangled near his shoulders, that at first glance might cause one to mistake his nature for more playful than it was. Cal would deem himself a proud mutt, but when you're head of the sole family of dogs to make their home in the Woods, you become *the* dog; the definition your face, your actions. All in all, it was a mixed bag—especially considering his past. When you grow up with an exiled raccoon with a penchant for poaching for a mentor, life in the Woods is an uphill battle. Cal clutched a makeshift fishing rod loosely in his paws—a slightly gnarled branch with a bit of moss-dyed twine and a rusted hook that he'd discovered, poorly hidden at the base of a nearby birch—and tried to focus on the soft draw of the passing current. It was as close to nothing as he could achieve in such a spot. He tucked his head to his shoulders and hunched over as the wind picked up, his shadow a curled leaf husk in the milky light of the moon. The late autumn air tinged with wood smoke and a crisp chill was enough to make him sniffle. In the twilight, the beauty of the woods around him slipped into darkness: the dogwoods, red oaks, and maples—his favorite— sporting limbs full of crimson and scarlet; groves of hickory and birch clinging to the last of their golden-yellow treasure; the elusive sumac— *her* favorite—too soon torn of its purple shade, a sight so painfully timed to make him almost chuckle.

But to laugh would be to consider more than the calm of the river. More than the lost beauty of the Woods. More than the bite that brought sickness to his dear Winifred, wife of never-enough years. The lies that he told his two pups when they woke to find their mother missing, Cal hurrying them off to school in the care of curious neighbors. The lies he'd tell them when they came home to find her still missing, Cal's words empty with false hope, prolonging the inevitable. The lies he'd tell himself at night under the stars, when loneliness takes hold and memories of a desperate search, of discovering her lost in the Fells, snarled lips caked in foam. He will remember so vividly the savagery in her eyes —and work tirelessly to re-convince himself that the mutt he loves is gone—and the violence of their last moment together, pistol impossibly warm through his coat against his fur, claws caked with burial mud, the numbness of the river, his late trek home. If it weren't for his boys, becoming lost himself might not be such a bad thing. All of this and more drifted through Cal as he watched the hook hover in the shallows, surrounded by fish too eager to run themselves through.

A splash gave him a start. An ancient catfish broke the surface of the river beside Cal's line, the fading light giving his back a slimy sheen that, combined with his wide-set eyes, gave him a grotesque swamp-creature look: out of place and well past his time. His whiskers like thick ropes grew wide across his upper lip before dipping low, disappearing into the depths. He hadn't strayed from the river's elbow in years (the current slow enough to allow him such bobbing pleasure) and unlike other fish, developed a penchant for talking to strangers, thus prolonging his life. For who would catch such a talking fish? Certainly not Cal, nor whomever the catfish first spoke to, nor (and perhaps they were one and the same) whoever gave the catfish the clever idea of calling himself Gil.

"I can talk all the trout on the river into jumping onto that hook, but if you're not going to put in the effort to bait it anymore, I'll just go back to sleep, thank you very much." Gil's wide lips sucked at the night air in soft wet smacks. If it weren't for the odd speech (and horrendously gummy accent), one might think he was making love to the night.

"It's cold for me to be up here, you know. I can feel it in the back of my throat." He stretched his mouth open, displaying his cavernous gullet as if Cal could somehow see his uncanny sense of temperature. "See? I'm going to catch a chill thanks to you."

"I thought that's what whiskers were for—keeping you warm." Cal felt a slight tug on the line and gently raised the rod in response, teasing the hook around whatever lurked below. The last fish he'd pulled in had somehow shot off the line and gotten lost in the dark. The three fish he'd stashed in the wood cooler he'd found alongside the old rod—two trout and a black crappie—were enough, and the longer he sat, the less energy he had to fight for another.

"My whiskers are teasing the bottom, telling my lips they'd be much warmer nestled in the mud."

"The decisions you face, Gil."

"Hey! My impulsive nature demands I entertain those who happen by this lovely spot on the river. It's the poor saps like you who abuse my gifts."

"I wasn't planning to stay. You're the one who pointed me to the fishing gear that had been left behind."

"We haven't seen each other in years! You're blaming me for wanting to catch up with an old friend? You have children! I had bet you the Woods would burn down in some horrible accident caused by one of those match-tossing badger boys, and I'd die a slow painful death while the river boiled my insides before I heard those words. Doesn't everyone want to talk about their kids? I actually want to listen! Your mate Roderick has twenty-six bunnies fighting each other for scraps of lettuce or whatever the hell they eat. I can't tell one from another, and I sometimes doze off halfway through, but I sure as mud float here while he's trying to remember them all. You've sat there for an hour and we've barely covered the weather! I should have saved pointing out the fishing gear for when the youngsters returned and given them a good scolding. At least they would have been entertaining."

"Rod's not my mate. You pointed out the fishing gear to me because you wanted someone to clean up after the rabbits. If you'd waited they would have ignored you, and the next time I came around I'd get a long, sad story about how your feelings were hurt, and how rabbits are nothing but a blight on the river."

"You're putting words in my mouth."

"Am I?"

"Yes. Well, all right, they still leave a mess behind and never clean up after themselves despite my pleas. Let me tell you, the lack of respect around here with the kids these days . . . "

Gil's monologue-turned-rant hit Cal like a nostalgic brick to the head, dislodging buried memories of lazy afternoons spent along the riverside—after he'd set traps and sent off the Rubbish Heap gang with bundles of hides and other contraband to be smuggled—a time he'd prefer stay forgotten after spending so much time and effort distancing himself from his previous life. But the days were a warm reminder of why he found himself at the river after wandering aimlessly for hours, and why, despite their differences, it was comforting to sit beside an old, often annoying, friend, especially when they are delighted to see you.

Now, dogs are known for their superior awareness, even the laziest of breeds—their ability to detect, track, and sense change is second to none, especially amongst the denizens of the crowded wood. This is especially true for Cal given his beagle-mutt inheritance. Despite his usually keen awareness, Cal didn't hear the bear coming. He froze with great terror, dropping his gnarled rod into the river with a start at the sight of the bear dashing into the river, sending water crashing in all directions as he snatched ol' Gil between his massive jaws.

Old Brown stood to his full monstrous height, lifting Gil high into the air, locked between his sharp teeth. Patches of missing fur and old scars that crisscrossed the elder bear's body were on full display as Gil flailed wildly, head and tail flapping against the bear's head. His mouth popped open again and again, but no sound came out, as if he'd regressed to mere catfish out of fear. Old Brown let out a harsh grunt, turned his head to the side and gave Gil a hard shake that brought instant submission. In the silence that followed, Cal feared the worst.

In a movement fluid from decades of practice, Old Brown clutched Gil between his claws removed him from his mouth and plopped down into the river, the displaced water rippling out against the banks, teasing Cal's feet. He held Gil inches from his face, the two staring at each other for what felt to Cal like an eternity, before the bear's lips parted to reveal a massive grin, and a deep laugh rumbled from his belly.

"I did it," he said, mid-chuckle. "The oldest pair this side of the mountain, face to face. I've been hearing rumors that you've been boasting of plans to outlive me. Calling it quite the

24

accomplishment for a fish. Thought I'd come down and see for myself. Maybe get lucky and settle the issue at hand."

Old Brown briefly turned his attention to Cal, giving him a wink. "Rare to find you out this way these days. You can relax, I'm not going to eat it . . . although," he said, returning to the catfish. "Winter is tickling the top of the mountain, and I am in no shape for a cold slumber. Skin and bones will just not do, and a nice fatty fish would buy me a few days."

He tilted the fish back and forth, giving each of his captive's wide-spread eyes an extended moment of petrifying horror. As Old Brown slowly lowered Gil back into the river, Cal couldn't think of a time he'd seen an animal take such pleasure in the torture of another, and though he'd brushed it off, it made part of him deeply worried. He clenched his jaw, willing himself to stay in place as his muscles tensed, ready for action. His fear turned to anger at his inability to have sensed the bear coming. Animals lived and died by their nose and ears. Distractions were just that, no matter how serious. There was no excuse to get caught flat-footed, ever—a lesson all dogs instinctively learn.

When Gil's gills passed below the surface, his mouth split open to a sickening width, as if he'd torn something within in an attempt to leap up and devour the bear's face, but instead formed an unnatural bugle to channel a nauseating scream. It was a sound reminiscent of a sheep bleating, frozen on one ear-splitting note, mixed with a rabbit's strangled death-wail, when its neck fails to break and it's partially eaten alive. A sound so awful it made Cal whimper and pull his droopy ears tight.

Old Brown ripped Gil back out of the water, holding him in place with one paw and clamping his mouth shut with the other. He bared his teeth, and reared his head back—and sneezed, spraying the catfish with thick mucus.

"If you ever do that again, I will tear off those whiskers, stuff them down that hell-hole you call a mouth, and leave you to suffocate in a tree while birds pluck out your eyes!" He roared at Gil, turned, and launched him upstream, sending the catfish soaring, fins outstretched, whiskers waggling behind. However, given Gil's awkward size, slimy skin and less-than-aerodynamic build, the aim was slightly off and Gil landed with a wet thud on the bank, half-bouncing, half-rolling back into the river. He disappeared without a peep below the surface.

"He'll be fine," Old Brown said, dismissing the poor throw. He dunked his paws in the river, rubbing the catfish filth from his palms before massaging his throwing shoulder. "These joints on the other hand. Remind me to warm up next time."

The movement of a cardinal caught Cal's attention as it flittered overhead, dancing between trees. He glanced up to find the moon had risen, and it was well past time he ventured home. The possibility of his boys, hungry and waiting for him to return, weighed heavily on his heart as the guilt continued to pile atop his shoulders. At least there would be dinner—the fish their first full meal in days. The thinnest of silver linings, if such things could be found during the worst of times.

Old Brown exhaled a heavy sigh. "Where were we?"

"I was just leaving." Cal stood, brushing bits of crushed leaves from his coat.

"Why not stay a moment and chat? I was never much for timing, and since I caught you out this way, it's the least you could do. A dog who can't pick up on an old bear must have a lot on his mind."

Cal shivered as the wind kicked up against his legs, and he made to stuff his paws inside his coat pockets. Old Brown grew tense in response, rising slightly out of the water.

"Keep those paws where I can see 'em. I can smell gunpowder on you. Since when did you become so careless?" He ran a finger along the left side of his jaw, calling attention to two lines of pale skin gouged through his dark coat, one leading to the ragged edge of his ear. "These scars—I spend too much time alone on the mountain to harbor a grudge. That's the sort of ill will that festers, poisoning beyond reason when bottled for long. I forgive, but I don't forget. I have more than a few of these thanks to you and those varmints. Sneaking cowards, the lot of them."

Cal's paw brushed against the pistol in his right pocket. He considered it for a moment before withdrawing, hanging a digit in the corner of the pocket. Far enough away to acknowledge the bear's warning, but close enough to pull, given their history. When Cal was a wee pup, he'd gotten lost in the Fells, separated from his parents. After wandering for days he was found by Maurice, a mangy raccoon who headed the Rubbish Heap gang, a band of rough-and-tumble vermin. To the dismay of many rodents, Maurice raised Cal as his own, giving him power over the rank and file. As Cal grew older, he eventually moved to the Woods, keeping his business with the Fells secret while becoming part of the community.

"I left the Rubbish Heap behind long ago," Cal said, scratching an itch underneath his chin with his other paw. "No doubt you know that. It was a means: nothing more, nothing less."

"Oh, your rift with Maurice and his boys was the talk of ages. Every squirrel, possum, and rat for miles came to tell me about Cal the honorable family dog, fighting back against the scavengers and smugglers. A knife in the back makes for furious gossip."

"I simply walked away."

"Nothing in the Woods is simple. If the blaze hadn't been such a distraction, your situation would be quite different, no?"

"A *distraction?* " Images of the fire burned through Cal's mind in a wave of unbridled rage. He felt the ghost of searing heat against his back, the smell of his own flesh cooking in the choking smoke. In the old schoolhouse, a hot coal had spit from the fireplace into a stack of papers at the back of the room. Before anyone could react, the entryway was engulfed in flame, trapping half the children inside, cut off from their classmates and teacher. Cal had been on his way home after a long day when he caught a whiff of the smoke and came running. Parents and bystanders looked on in horror as the fire licked around the outside of the building. The scared faces inside reminded Cal of his own when he was young and separated from his parents, lost in the Fells with only his reflection in the river for company. Cal's instincts kicked in and he threw himself through a window

RAGGED

to create an escape. He shooed two deer and a squirrel out who could walk on their own, and carried a pair of otters, siblings, who had temporarily succumbed to the smoke. Outside, parents threw dirt on his back and patted out his blackened fur to squelch the fire. Moments later, the roof collapsed, burying the school while the teacher took a headcount. Cal made it through the tense aftermath until all were accounted for, and promptly passed out.

"You—" Cal began, but turned away, clenching his teeth to cut himself off. The threats the bear had made to Gil were not empty, and to accuse Old Brown of cowardice, of abandoning the Woods— *his Woods*—at its darkest hour, would be to invite a grave reply. "Got yourself a pretty wife and a couple of pups for the effort," said Old Brown, continuing to prod.

Cal swallowed hard at the mention of Winifred, closing his eyes to fight off tears. He thought of the gun in his pocket, crusted with dirt, paw flexed at pocket's edge, curious if it would fire and pack enough punch to bring the bear down. The longer he took the bear's jabs, the more he felt the urge to stoke the fire.

"And you sit above us all in that cave and judge while we suffer. Why do you even bother to stretch your legs?"

Old Brown grunted and turned over onto his stomach, crawling toward the riverbank, his shoulders and head above the surface.

"This mountain is my home. These woods, my family. A band of weasels and stoats tearing the throat out of a defenseless deer and smuggling her remains down-river for sale doesn't concern me like it used to. Sure, I'd cull the pack when the gangs overstepped, but we're all savages at heart. A field mouse will sink its teeth into your flesh when it's cornered and starved.

"Outsiders concern me, Cal. *Disease* concerns me. And you possess the ripe stink of both. It's in your fur, your coat, your red eyes. The Woods has banished its own for less."

Old Brown burst from the river, paws outstretched for Cal, who was tense and ready this time, yet Old Brown's reach was too long and he snatched Cal by his coat as he tried to back away, popping a button loose, wrenching him to the river's edge, face-to-face. As Old Brown pulled him in, Cal ripped the pistol from his pocket, pulled back the hammer and pressed it into the side of the bear's skull. The rivals snarled, bared their sharp teeth with clenched jaws.

"Confident you could pull the trigger before I gnaw your face, Cal?" said Old Brown, pushing his forehead down against Cal's brow.

"I'm willing to chance it."

"It wouldn't look good—me in the river and you on the bank with half a face for the wife and kids to find. Horrifying picture, isn't it? Or would Maurice and his crew discover you first and make you disappear? A father abandoning his post."

Cal pressed the barrel against the bear's skull with renewed vigor at the mention of neglecting his kids.

"That's the spirit." With his free paw, Old Brown patted the earth beside Cal, groping around until a thick finger bumped into the wooden cooler. He knocked the container over, spilling the fish into the leaves. One by one he brought the fish to his mouth, leaves and all passing down his gullet. The first two he swallowed whole. The last, and largest, he tore into, flicking fish guts against Cal's chest as he severed the front half, letting the tail drop into the water, disappearing with a small splash.

Cal pushed off Old Brown the instant he felt the bear's grasp relax. Old Brown bellowed, his deep laughter echoing in the night as he slipped back into the river. Pistol pointed at the ground, paw flexed around the grip, Cal watched as Old Brown took his time, slowly trudging upstream and out onto the opposite side of the river where he shook, wringing water from his thick coat in all directions. He sauntered off into the woods, not once looking back.

2

Cal chewed on his tongue, listening to the bare tree limbs rattle in the wind. He stared after Old Brown, cursed him and his slow meander, and imagined the nub of his tail taunting him like a wagging finger with each step. A last laugh knowing there was little chance (especially given Cal's long distance from home) that Cal would snap, jump into the cold water with reckless abandon, and make the crossing to pursue him. But the exchange was only in his mind—the night playing a trick on his eyes, and when he blinked, the specter of Old Brown vanished into the dark.

"Serves you right for letting him get under your skin," Cal muttered out loud to himself, pawing the frayed threads where the bear's grip had torn a button from his favorite coat. As he contemplated the night, it struck him that Old Brown, like himself, knew more than he was letting on, and it was possible he might have been looking for Cal all along, making Gil a convenient distraction. The thought gave Cal a headache, mixed signals of fear and aggression washing over his brain. He stretched his neck skyward and howled, loud and long at the night, until his throat burned and his voice went hoarse.

"Damn you, Old Brown!" Cal snapped his arm out straight, and squeezed the trigger twice, wincing as each deafening blast rattled his body. The two rounds zipped aimless across the river into the woods, silent as to their final destination. Dropping to his knees, Cal slammed the pistol against the riverbank. The act jarred his numb fingers, and he whipped the weapon away in frustration. The trigger guard snagged his finger, sending the gun skittering over a series of thick tree roots, plunging it into a wild evergreen shrub. Cal took after the gun on all fours, calling himself a number of colorful, terrible things, and threatening, if he did not find the gun, to eat a bird-berry pie, a feat which would provide six days of immeasurable agony, followed by a total loss of bodily function and a most embarrassing death. Cal dug deep, the bush's dry foliage scratching at his face as he blindly floundered. Finally, after a pair of rotting fish heads, a red-and-white plaid kerchief (which he shook out and pocketed), and a rabbit-sized shoe (confirming once again that the entire species was an inconsiderate mess) he found what he was looking for. And before he could give it another thought, threw the pistol end-over-end into the river. The barrel caught the surface with a plunk, the weightier half dragging the gun below.

Cal watched the river for a moment to make sure it was gone, that Gil didn't pop up and return it in some perverse game of fetch. He knew it wouldn't come back—and it didn't—but the confidence provided no closure, instead only working to further the sense that he was a criminal hiding a terrible crime. And if he could have found it in himself to be honest, he was. After all, wasn't that why he'd dug up the gun after initially burying it near his wife? The way his paws throbbed with guilt after digging the shallow hole, the shame it brought on him to cover it up. When half your life is spent trapping fellow animals in the wilds of the Fells, it takes little to turn the Woods against you, and given the chance for anything to go sideways, for his pups to inherit his sins; he'd be forced to keep it to himself. And that was only the beginning, for as much as Winifred's death haunted Cal, the specter of her illness was that much worse, for it damned both the living and the dead. Old Brown set precedent decades ago when he initiated Maurice's exile—the Woods folk took care of their own, and any sign of serious disease or infection was met with swift action. It had taken Cal half his life to encounter Winifred. It meant the world to him to be with another of his kind. The fact that they fell in love, and that she was the most wonderful animal he'd ever met was flowers on the wreath. His pups deserved the community he never had—to enjoy their brotherly company free of hardship. Damn him if he let anyone take that away.

Out of spite Cal righted the empty ice box, replaced the cover, and took it with him. It was bulky, shifting against his hip as he walked, but weighed little without the fish Old Brown had stolen. He'd detour past the General Store on the way home and see if he could trade with Duchess for something to eat. The hedgehog drove a hard bargain, but the ice box was in decent shape, and on the off chance the kerchief went well with whatever apron she'd chosen for her shift, he might be able to work in an extra loaf of crusty bread for the effort. There were miles between his sore feet and home, but it was worth it— *if* the Two Old Cats caravan had come through with supplies. The wagon-bound trading company could not have chosen a worse time to run late. He left the river behind, one arm up to shield his face from branches as he made his way through a line of trees to a rock-strewn meadow. The moon lit up the small clearing, and helped him to navigate across to one of the small paths that had been well trampled under small feet. The Woods sprawled out before him, Old Brown's mountain at his back as he began his hike. When he was young and petulant, the mountain was an ominous sight, a shadow that grew out over the world each day, shrouding the Fells and giving poachers fits. But as he grew wise and traversed the trade routes, the mountain seemed to melt into the earth, a mere extension of the Woods, dwarfed by white-capped behemoths far in the distance.

Adjacent to the Woods proper, the Fells was an area that most settled animals spent little time in, if any, having been warned at a young age of the scavengers, *poachers*, who lurk in the dark, kidnapping children for the meat, skin, and bones. The stories held all the hallmarks of tall tales told to keep young ones in line, except it was all true—well most, anyway. The river served as a rough guide, as it marked the separation between the Woods and the Fells, where a rocky landscape dotted with all manner of boulder and jutting stone replaced the rich soil of the Woods, and yet somehow the trees grew thicker and denser, becoming almost claustrophobic at times. Cal used to take long walks alone through the Fells, especially in the spring, when all manner of fresh smells of growth and renewal sprouted from the earth, released by the rains and melting snow. It was his time to be alone, to get away from the rats, opossums, and weasels of the Rubbish Heap and be a dog. No matter how desperately he yearned for a family, he knew in his heart they were not meant to mix. But to banish memories meant to avoid those scents, and until tonight the closest he'd come to returning was when he'd taken his pups to the meadow, where he retold stories of the Fells meant to scare, though they instead brought intrigue, and he and Winifred had to be that much more vigilant. More than once Cal caught himself reminiscing at the scent of the pups' coats, their breath sour from cranberries when they'd come in from play, and it pained him to reprimand them in front of their friends.

Cal was still a good distance from home when he caught a whiff of warm, mushed carrots. The smell reminded him of his hunger and made him gag at the same time. Carrots were barely passable when consumed raw. When it came to root vegetables, he was more of a rutabaga fan. Nevertheless, the scent stuck with him—it stood out as odd to linger in such a time and place.

Cal backtracked several paces sniffing at the air, cautiously scanning the trees for movement. The scent led him back around a bend to a large bush, where to his surprise (and wonder at what else he might have missed along his journey toward home) he spotted a pair of muddied feet sticking out from beneath the foliage. In full view of the bright moon overhead, the bush was an exceptionally poor choice for a hiding place, having lost most of its leaves. Even with the splash of mud, he recognized the two missing toes on the rabbit's right foot. Cal shook his head. The rabbit in question was never known for making good decisions.

"Pssst," Cal whispered, taking a step closer to the bush. "Roderick, I can see you." The rabbit stood frozen in place, giving no indication of acknowledging Cal's presence. Puzzled, Cal placed the ice box on the ground, flicked one of the bush branches, to similar effect, until he finally grew impatient, bent down, and yelled into the bush.

"Hey, Rod! It's me, Cal!"

Roderick wiggled his feet in place, but still the rabbit remained behind his transparent camouflage. Cal cursed the night, ignored the dry limbs digging into his coat as he punched a paw into the bush, and clamped around Roderick's throat. The rabbit flailed in protest, violently shaking free the remaining leaves as Cal ripped him out. Roderick let out a choked cry, paws scratching at Cal's arm. The rabbit wore a thin green coat and a dark gray cap pulled down to his mouth that forced his ears back and down below his shoulders, with holes cut for his eyes and pink nose. A curious outfit—one quite different from Roderick's usual look, and it made Cal even more suspicious. When Roderick finally calmed, Cal set him down with a warning to stay put.

"Oh, hey, Cal. Funny seeing you out this way," Roderick said, voice wavering.

"Real funny. I've been getting that a lot lately. Why are you following me?"

"Following you? Wh-why would I do that?" Roderick massaged the sides of his neck, unable to make more than fleeting eye contact.

"You were standing in that bush."

"This bush? There are no leaves on this bush. Why would I hide in a bush with no leaves?"

Cal sighed, shook his head. "There—there were leaves on this bush until I pulled you out."

"You pulled me out? I must have dozed off. I was having the most curious dream—it was snowing—my feet were cold and I was trying to hide this burlap sack full of carrots that I'd come into possession of. They'd already been cleaned and smelled so juicy that I couldn't bear the thought of sharing with just anyone. The ground was too hard for me to bury them, so I found a big bush to tuck them under. That's when—out of nowhere, mind—a snake leapt into the bush and wrapped around me! It was a blur of white and red and so strong, but I fought against it with all my might and—" Roderick paused, sudden realization halting his train of thought with a nervous chuckle. "Oh, that must have been you. I'm afraid I got a bit carried away. Not sure what I'm getting at, other than that it's been a long day."

"That's one thing we can agree on. I'm cold and tired, and I'm not going to ask you again."

"Well, this time of night and all that. Shouldn't you be home with the kids?"

Cal clenched his teeth, a slight growl beginning to hum in the back of his throat. "Since when were you concerned with my kids?"

"Not me, never. I mean, I don't have many concerns outside myself, you know."

"Speak up!"

"I'm hungry, Cal!"

"So am I! We're all hungry."

Roderick leapt forward, thumping his paws against Cal's chest. "What happened to Winifred? Can you tell me so—"

A sudden current of adrenaline surprised Cal, his fur standing on end as if he'd dunked his head in the frigid river. "How dare you mention my wife! What's going on? Who's behind this? Answer me, damn it!" Cal forced Roderick back into the bush, pressing him against the brittle branches. The rabbit's mouth hung open as he stared wide-eyed with fear.

"Who *bit* my wife?" Cal barked through snarling jaws. He slammed the rabbit back into the bush. One of the thin branches snapped, plunging into Roderick's neck just above Cal's grip. The cut was small and unbeknownst to Cal, but deep, severing the carotid artery, and when Cal pulled him back out in frustration, the cut opened, spraying arterial blood over the left side of Cal's face.

"Oh—oh, dear," muttered Cal. He plugged the hole with his paw and stopped the flow as one last squirt hit his ear as he adjusted his grip. He stood frozen, unable to take his eyes off the slumping rabbit as the blood on his fur began to cool and the shock of the moment took hold. When the muscles in his arm began to tingle, he lowered the rabbit. He felt the neck twist as he did so, and a glance confirmed it was unnatural and broken, vertebrae bulging beneath the rabbit's thin skin. Still holding Roderick, he turned in place, looking around to see if anyone had witnessed their confrontation. Satisfied for the moment, he laid Roderick down at his feet and pointed the wound away from him, though he kept a foot next to his head to make sure he stayed that way.

"Blast." Cal made to wipe a sleeve against his face, but recalled the kerchief he'd found, and used it instead—though its lightweight material was a poor substitute and it smeared the rabbit's blood more than removed it. The rabbit had known something about Winifred and Cal was too stupid and angry to calm himself down . *If only she'd been here. Her lovely voice, her calming presence able to restrain me, I'd—*

No, it was too painful to consider now. Winifred's loss impacted every aspect of his life, but to reminisce now, in the moment, would be paralyzing. A disease spread by bite threatened the Woods, and it was bigger than Winifred getting sick. Something— *someone*—had brought it here, and damn him if she was going to take the fall. He had to find a way to stop it without exposing his family to the hysteria that walked hand-in-hand with rumor.

Now he had another mess on his hands. Roderick wasn't considered an upstanding citizen of the Woods by any means, and rabbits had a tendency to disappear on a regular basis, but he didn't need *another* mystery following him around.

What a day. He placed his paws on his hips, closed his eyes and stretched his weary back. When he opened his eyes he saw the ice box glowing in the moonlight. His ears perked up, and for the first time in what felt like an eternity, he had a plan.

Cal didn't want to leave the body, so instead of bringing the ice box over, he dragged Roderick down the path a short distance by his leg, his head bouncing over a pair of thick tree roots. When he'd lined the body up next to the ice box, his heart sank and he began to lose confidence in his plan. The rabbit was several inches longer than the box, his wide, padded feet and ankles jutting out past the side-handle. If only Cal could roll his legs up underneath him like his pup's winter socks, packed neatly in the bottom drawer. *Or a worm. A rabbit with worms for legs.* Cal shivered at the bizarre mental image. *Focus.*

He gave it a shot anyway. Cal lifted Roderick by his jacket and dumped him head first into the ice box. He took full advantage of the rabbit's broken neck, squishing him against one end, but still his legs and big feet (even with missing toes) wouldn't jam inside. Cal took a step back to consider the scene. He scratched his chin and remembered that there were few puzzles he was unable to solve. Like that time when he tied some oak sticks together with a bit of twine to form a raft for a crew of vermin to use along the river. The initial success led to the request of larger and more complex rafts, until the ill-fated maiden voyage of the *Fells' Swoop* resulted in the drowning of 32 rats after a run-in with a pair of vengence-hungry beavers.

There was more than enough room in the ice box—he just needed to take his time and not panic.

Taking hold of the Roderick's feet, Cal flipped him over and stuffed him rump down, contorting his legs up like a dead insect, his neck again at a sickening, unnatural angle that pushed his chin forward over his chest. Cal gave himself a premature pat on the back. The rabbit fit inside the ice box, but the lid wouldn't close over his head. Cal tugged off the rabbit's cap, thinking removal of the thin layer might be enough, but it only made it worse having to deal with his floppy ears.

Cal sighed, wringing his paws. *Of course*, he thought. *Nothing can be easy.*

Resigned to getting his paws dirty (or *dirtier*, as it may be) he glanced around once more to make sure he was alone before he bent and took the rabbit's neck between his jaws. Cal grasped its ears with one paw and bit down, his teeth punching through flesh. The rabbit's blood was sweet on his tongue and moistened his parched throat. With a quick torque, Cal separated the rabbit's head from its body, the crack of the neck bones alarmingly loud in the quiet night. He pressed against the severed head with both paws and used all his weight to squeeze it into the cooler, forcing it down toward the bottom. But the ears got in the way again and he cursed himself for removing the cap because there was no way he was going to get it back on the severed head. So, after attempting a number of obscene configurations that left Cal tired and the cooler sloshing with blood, Cal gave up, opting to take the body with him and toss the head. He heaved the rabbit's head by the ears as far as he could into the dark. The head made a wet thunk as it struck a nearby tree, bouncing deeper into the woods. He told himself later on the way home—straight home, the cooler and the kerchief now of questionable value—that the head likely landed in a leafless bush, in plain view for the next passerby.

3

It was well into the evening hours, the crickets and other musically inclined insects through tuning their instruments, when Cal finally dragged his aching feet up the porch steps and across the threshold of his family's log cabin. After his encounter with Roderick, he'd switched back and taken one of the longer routes along the mountain side of the Woods, following the river before cutting in when he hit new growth in the area of the Woods that fell to fire a decade ago. If he paid close attention, he could still pick up a hint of charcoal in a strong breeze. No animals inhabited the new growth—those who lost their homes rebuilt on the other side of the Woods, many with the purpose of being closer to the new school, which replaced the one that had been destroyed. The fire would have taken his home, too, if it weren't for the rains, which came hard and heavy just as the logs on the backside of the house were beginning to smoke. While another animal might have moved anyway, Cal found meaning in the building's salvation, and in many ways it was tied to his own at the time, the burn scars covering his back a constant reminder of the price.

Cal had lived in the small cabin since before he met and fell for Winifred. It had just enough room to give them each their space, but not so big to put them out of a few steps of one another. Cal stashed the ice box beneath his workbench out back, quickly washed up, and began to make supper. Winifred had always been a much better cook, and the pups had learned well from her teaching. They'd spent hours at her side during summers past, patient and eager to learn. Cal's inability to learn new tricks was a long-running inside joke that had been funny well past its expiration date. But as he looked over their collection of spices—her choice dried citrus peels hidden toward the back— his failure to channel any of her magic bit deep, making her loss loom heavy in the small home.

Soon a fire crackled in the hearth, warming the room. Above it hung a pot of thin stew consisting of mostly water, salt, pepper, dandelion greens, and thick, fatty chunks of rabbit meat. Cal added a pair of logs to the base of the fire and gave the stew a stir, tapping the spoon on the edge of the pot before giving it a lick. Bland was the best compliment he could give his cooking, but it would warm the pups' bellies and keep them nourished into the next day.

A bit of rabbit meat rose to the top, and he pressed it down with the spoon until it remained hidden in the murk. Cal preferred to remember Roderick as rabbit meat. The process of butchering him out back opened a door he couldn't close—sights and smells he would not soon forget, and so Cal felt better about the whole ordeal when it was just dinner. It wasn't that they didn't eat rabbit—after all, dogs need their protein—but the species was rare on their menu, usually when Cal stumbled on one that had recently passed or was injured, perhaps escaping the poachers, but in a bad way, and better that Cal end its misery.

While cooking wasn't Cal's forte, he was a pro when it came to butchery. His skill was well-honed from his youth running with the Rubbish Heap gang. Long afternoons spent alongside Maurice learning to properly flay skin, prepare meat and bone for trade, and get the highest return for their efforts when the poachers left for their smuggling routes. It wasn't the sort of thing he'd show off or do in the company of others, and it wasn't exactly what he'd describe as a *fun* process. But as he operated on Roderick and muscle memory took over, he felt the rush return. He'd have been lying if he said a small part of him didn't enjoy it, and he made short work of the rabbit to ensure it stayed that way.

After testing the stew, Cal pulled a bottle of applejack moonshine from a cabinet and poured himself a small glass. There wasn't much left in the bottle, and though it was uncommon for him to take a pull, he found himself itching for more. He took a sip. The golden liquid tasted sweet and refreshing, with only a hint of the high alcohol hidden within, going down like apple cider warmed in a kettle. Regal Toad's distant cousin, Figg, worked a distillery in a cranberry bog to the south. The off-kilter, mustachioed toad was a former bare-knuckle boxer who'd talk your ear off if you got too close—though as rabbits were to a good mess, toads were to a good chat. *One of these days*, Cal thought, *I should take the pups on a trip outside the Woods and pay him a visit.*

Cal was savoring the last sip when he heard yips of his pups closing in on the house, excited, no doubt, to check on their mother.

"Winifred . . ." A whisper of her name escaped his lips, and he looked out the window to see the moon staring down, high overhead. It was possible it appeared larger than when he'd been in the Fells, perhaps a bit more ominous, as if it had been looming over his shoulder while he'd busied himself, presenting harsh judgment over his neglect for his wife. It wasn't that he'd forgotten (how *could* he?) but in his hurry to prep for the pups' arrival, he'd forgotten to settle on his story about her whereabouts. She'd been present when the boys left for the day, but it was clear she was terribly sick—so sick that their youngest, Gus, threw a fit when he was marched outside and ordered to school. All he wanted was to stay home and help take care of his mother, and it tore at Cal's heart to be strict and refuse him.

In the short time it took Cal to get them dressed and across the Woods to the school house, Winifred had disappeared. Cal returned to find the cabin an empty mess, partially sacked as if someone had gone through their things in a hurry. A jar containing his collection of river stones lay smashed beside the fireplace, the smooth baubles scattered across the floor among piles of clothing, blankets, and other trinkets that had been ripped from their proper place. The corners of each rug had been pulled up, the dust underneath kicked about. At a glance, nothing appeared to be stolen, and he'd immediately dismissed the idea of a kidnapping—there were no odd or foreign scents in the home. Before he left to look for her he'd pried up a loose section of floorboards in their bedroom to check his hiding place, withdrew and pocketed his pistol. It didn't hit him until he saw her state that she must have torn the house apart searching for the gun, and it had nearly broken him to understand that he wasn't supposed to see her this way. She must have known what was coming, and wanted him to have no memory of her dire fate. But now she was gone, dead and buried, the gun lost to the river, and he the only one left who knew the truth, as dark and shameful as it was. And two loving, eager pups who wanted answers.

Fear arced along Cal's spine and a moment of overdue panic belted him in the gut. He dropped his glass on the counter and hurried across the room, painfully checking a hip against the dining table. He ripped open the door, made it down the steps around to the corner of the house before he fell to his knees and retched golden bile, the alcohol coming up neat, just as it had gone down. When he finished, he found the bloodied kerchief in his pocket, unwrapped a clean corner, and dabbed his mouth.

"You feeling all right?" Cal heard Billiam call out. The badger maintained a healthy habit of impeccable timing.

"I've had better days." Cal coughed, turning away as he stood to loosen a wad of phlegm.

"Sounds like a personal problem," Billiam said.

Cal nodded, acknowledging his friend, though unprepared to humor him at the late hour. He grimaced at the lingering taste, rolling his tongue over his teeth. The badger kept his distance as he sauntered up to Cal in his traditional crumpled suit, his fur disheveled, in need of a good grooming. If one didn't know Billiam, the "useless clerk" elected by the citizens of the Woods (SOLE ELECTED official, as he was wont to remind) to organize functions (and thus the target of general complaint), one might think his appearance was the result of long hours and the stress of a worrywart, but the badger looked the same at sunrise, which only made him the target for further ridicule. Cal would feel for his dear friend if the badger hadn't worked so hard to get himself the position in the first place.

Cal kicked at a nearby root, stuffed his paws in his pockets, but kept his head up in the hope of disguising his misery. "Boys around?" he said.

"Chasing each other in the woods. Should be around here, somewhere. I brought some molasses chews for the kids while they worked on their projects for the Moon Festival. Thought it might help them focus but most gobbled them up and spent the evening high on sugar."

"Appreciate you looking out for those two."

"No sweat, but you've got to get me a little notice up front. The missus is wrangling starving twins and Junior is giving us attitude. I'm going to catch hell when I get home."

"I know. I'm sorry. I'll make it up to you."

"Don't kid yourself." The pair turned their attention to the nearby sound of rustling bushes and trampling of leaves.

"How's Winifred feeling? One of the boys mentioned she was under the weather."

Cal felt the blood drain from his face and took a step back to steady himself. He'd been so focused on protecting himself that he'd forgotten the pups witnessed the sickness develop as well, and might not be as keen to hide it. He opened his mouth to respond when Gus burst through the trees.

"Beat you!" he yelled back over his shoulder at his brother. He sprinted straight for Cal, pack bouncing wildly on his back. "Catch!" he said, launching into the air, slamming into Cal's midsection, wrapping his small arms around his father in a tight bear hug.

"Hey, Pops! Mom home? Is Mom better?" Gus said, craning his neck up to peer at his father, then around him at their home and the dim oil-light within. Cal cringed at the mention of their mother being ill.

"Now wait just a second," Cal said as he pried his youngest off. "I want you to thank Mr. Billiam for—"

Franklin, the older of the pair, slipped past him with a short "Hi, Dad," and bounded up the stairs into the house. Gus yelled after his brother, charging unfairness and other brotherly complaints. He dropped down from Cal, made to chase after his brother before he stopped short and turned back, pulling a large painted cutout from the back of his head over his face, a bit of yarn on each side holding it in place.

"Check out my mask! I'm an owl," Gus said, mimicking a long owl's hooooo. The pup's mask for the Moon Festival was the very definition of festive, each feather painted with an unnatural array of colors—blue, pink and yellow melting

51

together in a disorderly pattern. Cal crouched and hugged Gus tight, eliciting a "Daaaaad." The pup was immensely proud of painting within the lines.

"Franklin made a raven but it's still wet so he left it at school," Gus said.

"No, I just didn't want to bring it home," Franklin shouted from within the cabin.

"Nutbrown said he's slow because he talks too much," Gus whispered with a tattletale's smirk. Nutbrown was a wise, matronly squirrel who'd taught the pups since before they were old enough to sit in a chair and pay attention. As wise as she was, she possessed an old habit of talking out of turn, and the pups took pleasure in relaying what kernels she let slip about the other.

"Your brother is a popular fellow," Cal said, and he wasn't lying. The boy was growing too fast.

Franklin popped his head out the front door. "Where's Mom?"

"Take your brother inside, wash up and wait for me." Cal gave Gus a pat on the rump and shooed him toward the house. "Dinner is almost ready."

"We get dinner?" Gus's eyes lit up. Cal could hear his youngest's stomach growl as the pup sniffed the air.

"Rabbit stew?" Gus's jaws overflowed with drool. He licked his lips and ran for the house, forcing his way in past his brother, who gave him hell for the effort.

"Rabbit stew?" Billiam echoed. Cal had almost forgotten the badger was there. Before he could speak to the question, the badger waved him off. "It's fine. It's fine. Don't need to know anything more than I already do."

"Where's Mom?" Franklin repeated.

"She's fine, Franklin. Go back inside," Cal said.

"I didn't ask how she was doing." Franklin's words dripped heavy with pre-teen attitude.

Cal held up a paw to silence his pup, nearly baring his teeth in anger as he stared him down. "Not another word."

Franklin rolled his eyes, disappeared inside, and let the screen door slam behind him.

"The mouth on that one, eh?" Billiam rubbed his paws together. "The way the missus steps on me, I'm bound for the same, if not worse." Billiam exhaled a long sigh.

"Rabbit stew! We really *are* having dinner!" Gus shouted from inside. He ran to the front and pressed himself against the window, giving Cal an excited thumbs up.

"Peas and rice, Cal. You're lucky you don't have a warren next door." Billiam scratched at the fur around his shirt collar. "Do you have a warren for a neighbor?"

"It's a long story," Cal said with a shrug.

"Say no more. As clerk I was never here—"

"—in an official capacity." Cal interrupted. "Yeah, yeah, plausible deniability and all that. You'd have to be blind to maintain that kind of innocence around here."

Billiam scoffed at the idea. "You're lucky I'm easily lonesome and fond of friends. Please give Winifred our best. Never a good time to be sick."

"Nothing to worry about, really." Cal cleared his throat to hide the anxiety creeping into his voice. "A simple cold, but I appreciate the concern."

The pair said their farewells and parted ways, Cal promising to have the kids ready on time in the morning for their usual walk to school. Since the fire and rebuilding of the school across the Woods, the west side animals had organized (with the assistance and blessing of Clerk Billiam, of course) a daily gathering where parents brought their children shortly after sunrise to commute to school. It began as a safety measure to give the young ones a bit of comfort, and continued as a routine. The kids were afforded time to goof off and parents got their fix of news and town gossip. The morning walk home was one of Cal's favorite times of day, when he and Winifred would take a long route, relaxing in each other's company, often holding paws in silence and taking in the wonders around them. She had an eye for spotting rare wild flowers, and on cool summer days she would pluck a bouquet. Once home, she'd place the collection on the kitchen table in one of several decorative vases. The flowers would fill their home with a wonderful fragrance for a week. In the moment, as he watched the badger leave, he thought he felt the ghost of her paw rubbing against his own, but the evening breeze rose and washed the sensation away, and when he clenched his paws seeking hers, he discovered them both empty, save his own rough palms. Cal took a deep breath, and ascended the steps to his home.

* * *

Inside he found little relief, the dry heat emanating from the hearth engulfed his senses, tickling his nostrils and stealing the moisture from his sad eyes. Cal closed the door, and slid the wooden bolt across the scarred frame. The pups sat at the dinner table, Gus with his paws in his lap and Franklin's knuckles bracing his chin, elbows on the table. They'd thrown their backpacks aside and hastily set the table with bowls, spoons, and napkins for four. Whether out of habit or hope, the presence of Winifred's setting made Cal wince, which he aimed to hide by turning away, unbuttoning his coat, and hanging it up beside the door. When Franklin opened his mouth to speak, Cal cut him off.

"Hold your tongue," he said. "We can talk while the stew cools." He regretted the gruff tone at once, and gave each boy a squeeze on the arm as he passed, thanking them for setting the table. Cal collected the bowls, carrying them one by one to the hearth. With a large wooden ladle, he filled each to the brim and set them on the table in front of the pups with a warning, if the steam wasn't enough, to be patient. The pups dug in anyway. They lifted greedy spoonfuls to their lips and blew on the chunks of rabbit, careful not to exhale too strongly and spatter the greasy liquid. When Cal returned to the pot a third time with his own bowl, his stomach, already twisted with anxiety, reminded him of the stew's contents, and he retreated to the counter with an empty bowl. With a rag he retrieved the pot while the pups slurped and placed it on a thin piece of cork to cool, and before he sat, poured himself another drip of the applejack, even though he knew it was poor judgment on his part—on his tongue still lingered the taste of bile.

"This is delicious, Pop!" A thin line of liquid dripped down Gus's chin as he spoke between bites. "Why don't you have some?"

"Manners. Finish up; it's past your bedtime." Cal retrieved the napkin that had fallen to the floor and placed it on the table beside his youngest. "I had my fill while preparing the meal, thank you."

Cal took his usual seat across from Franklin and set the glass down in front. Again, the boys eyed his lack of food. Cal wished he'd never poured the drink, but now that it was before him, he didn't want it to go to waste, either. After a moment of silence, Franklin perked up and locked eyes with Cal.

"So?" he asked. When his father did not immediately reply, Franklin pushed back from the table, arms hugged tight across his chest, spoon adding emphasis as it clattered in his near-empty bowl. It was clear he'd run out of patience, his anger just shy of an audible growl. It was a line which, if crossed, would force Cal to act as the family alpha to keep his pups in check. It wasn't a position he'd enjoyed as they'd grown older—he recalled his own father wrestling him to the ground, jaws clenched just so around his neck to make him heel.

"Right," Cal fidgeted, unable to find a comfortable position in his chair. *Winifred*, he thought. Oh, how he needed to tell them, to somehow explain in a way that might make sense of the tragedy—not only to them but to himself as well. And yet, to tell them would be to risk their future—any slip in front of the wrong friend or neighbor could land them in permanent exile. Every answer gave birth to more questions, surfaces he'd barely scratched. He couldn't find the words or where to begin, and as he felt a tickle tease the back of his throat and his pulse began to quicken, he knew that he'd buckle before he could utter a complete sentence. Perhaps on another night he'd be inspired to attempt to bring truth and closure to their family. But with wounds as fresh as the soft, turned earth, he found himself unable to focus, suddenly fixated on Gus's owl mask that he'd ditched beside his bag, and the words tumbled out of him to fill the void.

"How's the preparation for the festival?"

Gus piped up, mouth full. "We finished most of the decorations for the stage, but Mr. Billiam said it was too windy to hang them up. Plus, he said it was going to rain, which would ruin the streamers."

"Rain, huh? We're overdue."

"Mr. Billiam licked a finger, held it up in the air and said the breeze told him so. Can you do that? Junior said the trick was for show—that it really was his dad's bad knee acting up."

"Where. Is. Mother?" Franklin asked, calm and deliberate with a slight quiver.

Cal's paw shook as he brought the moonshine to his mouth, but as the glass touched his lips he felt a sickness threaten to bubble up, and he returned the glass to the table, paw to his lap to hide his tremble.

"Your mother is very ill," he began. "We felt there wasn't time to wait for the traveling doctor so she went over the hills to look for Ashbury. You both were probably too young at the time to remember the old dog, he—"

"Why aren't you with her?"

"I paid her a visit after dropping you off this morning. She left during the night." The half-truths triggered a flood of memories—sweat, smoke, heartbroken sorrow, of brushing a paw against his love's cheek one last time before sweeping dirt over her shallow grave—that forced Cal to clench his jaw and look away.

"Is she going to be okay?" blurted Gus, his eyes beginning to well with concern. Below the table Cal reached across and squeezed Gus's paw.

"How long will she be gone?" asked Franklin.

"We should all be with her," added Gus.

"You know she'd want you to continue your schooling."

"She's not coming back, is she?"

"What do you mean she's not coming back?" Tears slid down Gus's cheeks.

"What do you think I mean, muttface?"

"Franklin." Cal glared at his oldest, a look that he not dare utter another word.

"She's not, is she?"

"Franklin!"

Franklin stood, knocking his chair over in a rush, hiding his face as he hurried for the back, throwing open the door and escaping into the night. The door slammed behind him, jarring Cal's nerves and teasing his rage, but he knew it was more the wind's doing than his son's, and he let it go. To project blame on his innocent pups would drive a wedge between them that might never be overcome, and the longer he withheld the truth, the stronger the coming storm grew, and the stronger he'd need to be to weather it.

Gus howled, his face in his arms on the table as the tears began to flow in heavy sobs. Cal placed a paw on his back, softly rubbing in a circle across his shoulders. Gus turned away, burying his snout deeper beneath his arm to cover his eyes, which Cal was thankful for as he felt a tear escape and run down his own cheek. His desire to appear strong, to flex his muscles and hold the fraying threads together waned as the day took its toll, exhaustion mounting to the point of surrender. Wiping away his own tears, Cal hugged his son's back, whispered that his brother didn't mean those words, that they were going to be okay, that their family was going to be okay. Gus nodded and breathed deeply, and when he calmed, Cal instructed him to wash up, pull on his pajamas, and bed down by the fire.

"I'm going to get your brother." Cal kissed the top of Gus's head. "We'll be right outside."

Cal placed his glass on its side in the sink, watched the liquid trickle into the drain, and headed for the door.

* * *

Outside, the night air bit into his fur, and Cal wished he'd grabbed his coat to share with his son. Franklin sat where Cal knew he'd be—hugging his knees, his back against a clump of birch trees protecting him from the wind. It had been his hideout, his escape from the world since he'd been very young. When it became too easy to find him, he'd learned to climb. Franklin would climb up as high as the trees could support him, and out along limbs that swayed in the breeze under his weight. At the peak of his adventures he'd disappear for half a day, driving his parents mad until the sun set, and he'd call for help getting down.

"Room for me?" Cal kept his distance as he approached. He wanted to give his son space. Franklin turned his head away. He rubbed his eyes but remained seated, which Cal took as an invitation, sidling up next to him, careful to avoid the knobby roots that spread out beneath them.

"Did I ever tell you I first met your mother at a Moon Festival? It was cloudy like tonight, the full moon barely visible in the sky. I remember it was so dark that Duchess brought out jars packed with fireflies from the South and scattered the glowing beacons among the tables where the woods folk clustered, dancing and listening to the band.

"The crowd had momentarily thinned while parents chased their little ones home. She was standing at one of the tables off to the side of the stage in a silvery-white dress that sparkled in the dim glow. Can you guess what type of mask she wore?"

"A fox," Franklin mumbled.

"That's right. Has she told you this story?"

Franklin shook his head no. "I found it hanging on the inside of the closet door when I was little. I think it scared me. She told me it was from when you first met."

"A white fox." Cal chuckled. "There was something . . . off about it. Basic with no paint. It was bright and stood out—and not just to me. You know you're not supposed to think about what kind of animal hides behind the mask—that's the purpose of having fun and picking something different: an owl, a moose, a fox . . . "

Cal trailed off, not mentioning or explaining his own mask, a black sheep with a touch of gray on the nose that had been lost to time. A tongue-in-cheek joke that Maurice and the rest of the Rubbish Heap found hilarious, as Cal was the only one of their membership to live among the "civilized" Woods. To everyone at the Moon Festival it was just a poor mask that showed little effort and gave others little reason to engage him.

"Anyway, a pair of foxes approached your mother during a break in the music and confronted her over the mask. Made a big scene over a dog pretending to be a fox. That the mask was an insult to their kind."

"What did you do?"

"Feeling a bit lonely as I was, I took the opportunity to stroll over and give them a piece of my mind, a lesson on festival etiquette and how to treat a lady."

"What happened?"

"Thankfully they backed off to prevent any scuffle, and the band started back up, covering their exit."

"And then you met Mom?"

"Not quite. When I turned back from the music she was gone from the clearing, ran off into the tree line. I looked and looked, but it was so dark I couldn't follow. Then a sliver of moonlight cut through the clouds, illuminating her mask in the distance. She'd been watching me from afar, and as the moon slipped back, she lifted her mask and I caught a glimpse of her darling nose.

"I've been chasing her ever since."

Cal put an arm around Franklin and hugged him. Gone was any thought or words of wisdom or comfort, but for a moment Cal felt a spark crackle in his cold chest. A sense of hope that they might make it through to the other side intact.

"Remember, I spent most of my life without any fellow dogs for company. Always be there for your brother. I can't tell you how wonderful it is for you two to have each other. You won't realize it now, but Gus adores you—even when he's prodding and poking and being annoying."

Franklin leaned against Cal, and took a deep breath that turned into a yawn.

"Come on," he said. "Let's go inside and warm up."

Franklin rested his head against his father's shoulder and together they stood up, shaking out their coats as they pressed through the cold.

4

When the rains came, the clouds opened over the Woods and fat drops thudded against the cabin roof like a shower of acorns. While the pups pawed their way through dreamland, Cal lay belly-up and stared at the darkness spread across the ceiling, his ears alert and tuned in. He was attempting to distinguish a steady drip of water plunking softly against the floor boards from the cacophony outside. A low rumble of thunder had woken him, and once the drip caught his attention, he'd been unable to block out the distraction. He shivered as he stood, searching the immediate vicinity, in the dim light, for the source. The fire had died down considerably, and Gus had stolen Cal's third of the blanket at some point in the night. Cal yawned, feeling barely rested, though a glance at the antique clock on the wall beside the fireplace told him he should feel otherwise. Wellpast midnight, hours since he'd bedded down—Franklin closest to the fire with Gus between them. Not a word uttered, after they'd come inside, until Cal's whisper of goodnight, though Franklin appeared to be already out, breathing a light snore the moment he snuggled up to his brother.

Cal was quiet as he spread the bunched areas of the blanket over the pups, tucking their feet in. He stood and looked down at them as he stretched his sore limbs. The pair appeared smaller underneath the blanket, huddled close like they always were when very young, inseparable from almost the moment Gus was born. Now that Franklin was older he wasn't keen to be around his brother, though Cal knew—hoped—that phase would pass.

Cal made his way through the house, stepping softly around creaking floor boards, careful to avoid tripping over the pups' school bags. After scouring much of the room for the leak, he caught a glimpse of a splash on the table, and discovered a small puddle had formed between the settings he'd neglected to clear out of exhaustion. From the kitchen he took a small pot and a dirty rag, still damp from dinner prep. He gave the table a quick wipe, maneuvered the pot underneath the leak, and dropped the towel inside to muffle the sound. Satisfied after a few drops landed gently on the rag, he cleared the kids' bowls from the table and pondered working the fire before deciding that he'd be warm enough if he left the pups to enjoy their blanket and found his own.

A strong gust of wind shook the cabin. The branches of a scrawny pine scratched at the window beside Cal as he scoured the closet for another blanket. The sound drew a tingle up his spine that prickled his fur as he imagined someone testing the window, claws moving about the edges of the sill. He shamed himself and his imagination for giving the storm life, and yet, silly as it was, after he found the second blanket, he stood at the window and waited for another gust to drive the branches into the window and put his mind at ease.

"You're being ridiculous," he whispered to himself aloud. If anything, he should be worried about the shape he left the linen closet in after retrieving the blanket. Another painful reminder that he'd continue to find his wife in all things, though he couldn't help crack a smile at the thought of the hell he'd catch if she'd seen the disorganized state he left it in after fumbling about half-blind. He wrapped the blanket around his shoulders like a large shawl and looked out the side window toward the front of the house. Wide puddles dotted the now-muddy path where earlier he'd conversed with Billiam. Here and there small branches littered the path, but aside from the leak, it wasn't the type of storm to lose sleep over. Seconds ticked by, the blanket growing heavy, pulling him toward the hearth and rest he desperately needed. At last another gust swept against the cabin. Cal pressed close to the cool glass to observe the pine rock toward the window, listening to the tick-scratch-tick of its branches. Still, something pulled at him, a nagging fear that kept his feet glued in place. He squinted, cupping his paws around his eyes to block influence from the fire light behind him. A low growl grew in his throat as he scanned the dark. Nothing. *Go back to bed, you—.* Then, a flash of light. A distant bolt of lightning or a shift in the clouds revealed an unfamiliar shape—a shadow out of place among the brush.

There, at the tree line, closer to the front of the house. Someone—*something*—stood, watching him. A hint of dull white in the shadows surrounding an unblinking eye. Cal ran to the front of the house, threw himself against the window beside the door, teeth bared, paws and forehead pressed against the glass, protective instinct overriding all sense. He fought the urge to rip open the door and sprint into the night, barking incessantly at the unknown threat.

You're *dreaming*. He bit down on his tongue, hard, until he tasted blood, certain the pain was real.

You are *not* dreaming. He winced and sucked at the wound, his eyes continuing to adjust as he looked out over the porch, and when another flash came, he witnessed the thing again, closer now, creeping toward him across the muddy clearing. Soaked to the bone, its head lopsided and grotesque. A nightmarish version that shocked his senses, calling back to the night he met his wife. A hunched thing with a stretched and bloodied face.

"This can't be. This can't be," he repeated as he grabbed for his pea coat. With one sleeve on he opened the door and stepped out into the storm. The porch protected him from the worst of the rain, but a cold mist caused him to squint and shield his face to breathe. He pulled the door shut and faced the darkness, clutching his coat shut tight over his chest, no time to fumble with the buttons.

"Who's there?" he called. "Show yourself!"

Something round hurtled toward Cal's left. It rebounded off the side of the house and landed on the porch with a wet thunk. He crouched down to examine the object. It appeared roughly round at first, like an under-inflated leather ball, but when he poked at it with a paw he knew otherwise, and he took a step back from the threat. A small severed head lay on its side. It had been expertly skinned, leaving it devoid of features except for the vacant eyes, which thankfully stared away from Cal at the porch floor, for he almost instantly recognized them.

Cal heard the sound of footsteps in the mud and he rose to his feet with a snarl, growling, ready for a fight. A plump figure approached with a slight limp. Two white ears dangled to the side of its head, off kilter like a long, gnarled stem atop a demonic jack-o'-lantern. The thing began to laugh, and Cal knew.

"Maurice," Cal growled through clenched teeth.

The mangy raccoon stopped before him at the base of the steps, ankle-deep in muck, too-short burlap pants pulled up high on his waist, tied around with rough string through which he'd stuffed his old knit cap beside a well-worn sheathed blade. He'd skinned Roderick's head in mostly one piece, pulling the hide over his own like a grotesque burglar mask, though his own head was much larger, so the skin was stretched, tearing half-way up the side. The eye holes were mostly where they should be—canted over to fully reveal the raccoon's good left eye, but less so the scarred, eye-patched right. The hole for the rabbit's nose fell above his own giving the impression of two large perpendicular nostrils, and the mouth fared no better, scrunched tight below, hanging out like a too-small-shirt pulled over a belly, giving him a second, thin-lipped mouth, or a strange, hairless pink mustache. It had been years since Cal would have found this sight to be hysterical, but as awful as the past day had been, it almost did strike him as humorous to see it take another dark turn. His past, no matter how recent, seemed determined to haunt him.

"You should have seen your face," Maurice said. "A moment of pure shock and disgust. Dare say I think you've changed, old dog. On my stroll over I thought you might be attempting to get back into the game. Unfortunately, with the passage of time it would appear you have forgotten much of my teaching— leaving one of the tastiest morsels behind, stinking of dog. Tracked your kill right to your doorstep." Maurice winked with his good eye. "It'll be our little secret."

"What do you want?"

"I find it very curious . . . two days ago some of the boys told me they saw your wife sticking her pretty little nose around the Fells. I was quite proud of them for keeping their distance given our history. *Then* I get a report of *you* lurking around the Fells this evening. What am I to make of this? Perhaps I'm mistaken, hmm?" He performed a little jig, turning his head side to side, making the rabbit ears flop back and forth over his head. "What do you think? Not bad for a little late-night fun. The boys do most of the work these days but I still got *it*."

"You're not welcome here," Cal scolded the old raccoon, his anger hiding the sudden anxiety roiling his gut at the mention of the boys—Maurice's gang of stoats, weasels, rats, and other castoffs—observing his grief-stricken wander. What had they seen and when? A dozen questions fought to spill from Cal, but to show even a hint of curiosity would be to invite two-fold from

Maurice, whose nature was to latch on like a steel trap until the truth was freed—or the leg severed.

"Me?" Maurice pointed at his head. "Or this cat? I mean, rabbit. Ha! That was a good one.

"Aren't you going to ask me what I've been up to? It's been a while since we've seen each other eye to *eye*." Maurice paused a beat, pointed out the eye patch. "Get it? Sometimes it's me against the world out there. You seem to be doing well."

"I'm going inside," Cal said, turning to leave.

"You never liked my jokes. One positive result of your desertion—the rats have a terrific appreciation for my humor, and there are a lot more of them now. Though the chattering sound they make . . . now that I think about it, I sometimes miss being the only one to laugh." Maurice set foot on the bottom step. "Can I come in? It was a long walk to get here on these old legs."

"No, and get your muddy foot off my step."

"Not even out of this rain? I'm liable to catch a cold if I don't warm up soon. Eating garbage does wonders for the immune system but not in ways you'd think."

"No. Now get lost."

Maurice backed up into the muck, shoulders drooped, beaten, twiddling his claws. "Before you go, since I came all this way . . . do you think if I wore this to that festival of yours I could pass muster? Perhaps if I lost some weight and practiced hopping about."

Cal sighed, took a moment, closed his eyes. It had been years, close to a decade since he'd run across his old partner. As much as he hated the raccoon, he wouldn't show up without a reason. "Why? What does it matter?"

"The smell would give me away, wouldn't it? The delectable Rubbish Heap too fresh for you proper Woods folk. One of these years I'll pay a visit! We're not getting any younger, you know."

Cal stepped forward to the edge of the porch, rain falling an inch from his nose. Maurice took a step back in response.

"Oh, Cal. It's not every night that you find a delicious severed head hiding in a shrub. I thought for the special occasion I'd pay my old friend a visit, that's all. A coincidence by my mind— sometimes one thing just leads to another, right?" Maurice gave Cal a wink with his good eye. "Glad to see you still scare well after all these years."

"You're lucky my pups are inside, because if they weren't I'd come down there and drown you face-down in that mud."

Maurice feigned a gasp. "Calvin, is that the way you treat your guests? What if Winifred were to witness such a display of savagery? You made no mention of her—she's not sick, is she? I've heard—"

"What have you heard?" Cal jabbed a paw at Maurice as he pursued him into the storm, a spike of cold lancing up each leg as he stepped off the porch into the mud. "Answer me, damn it!"

"*There's my old friend.* Fresh wounds and raw nerves." A grin spread wide across Maurice's face, and Cal realized he'd lost control, falling for the raccoon's guile. "Nothing concrete, of course. Seems to be a sickness about. And you know how your fellow woods folk treat their sick . . ."

Maurice swept an arm out to the side and took a short bow. "Once marked with disease, always marked with disease, no matter the outcome. You can live, but you can't go home. If someone of import were to find out, that is . . ."

Cal locked eyes with Maurice, teeth clenched, muscles taut, burning with restrained rage and weighing options from murder to retreat with equal consideration. After a tense moment, he capitulated to his need to know more about what happened to Winifred.

"What is this sickness you speak of?"

Maurice perked up. The raccoon shuffled his feet to the right to look past Cal. "Well, it would appear we have an audience," he said, giving a little wave.

Cal started, spun to find the front door ajar, Gus clutching the heavy blanket. "Dad?" he said, rubbing sleep from his eyes.

Cal felt his feet sink into the mud, stuck as he was torn in each direction between the mystery of Maurice's appearance and the need to protect his son. When Winifred was first pregnant with Franklin, Cal had made a promise to himself (and to her) to shield their pups from his past life in the Fells. Nothing stayed hidden forever, that much was certain, but he'd be damned if he was going to let Maurice or any of the Rubbish Heap gang endanger his family. Since then he'd made amends and maintained control over his story for so long that it almost felt unreal to think back on those days. Now, standing there alone in the rain, it felt like cupping his paws together to catch the water, watching it leak through, disappearing in the wind.

"Go back inside, son. *Now*," he barked.

"Who are you talking to?"

"No one. Go snuggle up next to your brother."

Gus yawned, still in the doorway. "Is mom back?"

"Young ones," Maurice clicked his tongue against the roof of his mouth. "Such innocence. You never know when they're going to pop in and brighten your day."

Cal stomped up the steps, shaking filth from his feet, shooing Gus inside the house. After securing the door he listened for Gus's footsteps as he tip-toed back to bed, then turned to confront Maurice.

"Can I have my head back?" Maurice asked. "I put a lot of effort into this charade."

Cal gave it a swift kick, sending it bouncing down the steps to the raccoon's feet where it landed with a loud splurch.

"Ugh, now it's all muddy."

"Like that's ever stopped you before."

"Who said it was for me?" Maurice produced a small sack from a rear pocket, clutched the mess of a head, and stuffed it inside.

"Maurice," Cal called after the raccoon, desperately wishing for the pistol he'd so recklessly tossed away, if for nothing more than a threat to give his old friend pause.

The raccoon twisted the end of the bag close and tossed it back over a shoulder. "Goodnight, Cal. Be seeing you."

"Maurice!"

"Go back inside and tend to your family, Cal. As you said,

it's rare for me to be in these parts and I'm not one to travel lightly—or alone."

Cal slammed a fist into the porch railing. He'd been so focused on Maurice and his macabre stunt that he hadn't paid attention to the surroundings, and as the raccoon disappeared into the trees, he saw half-a-dozen or so pairs of yellow eyes among the shadows focused in his direction. Cal stared back, defiant, swallowing his urge to howl and charge into the woods after them. Maurice knew more than he was letting on, and Cal had inadvertently added to it. He had a lot of ground to cover, and there would be no sleep.

* * *

Maurice took a seat on a half-rotted stump and massaged the rough pads on the bottom of his weary feet. The rain had slowed—the worst of the storm blew over while he was still making his way through the Woods, and though the Rubbish Heap was close by, he needed a short rest. Soon after departing Cal's home, he'd sent his escort on ahead. Four rats, two stoats, and a weasel—all young and eager to please (and much quicker than he). There was work to be done: traps to be checked and reset; hides in need of leathering, bones of boiling. Besides, he needed some time alone to process the encounter. The rats had bickered with the stoats every step of the way over stepping on a stick, or some nonsense that occurred back in the Woods that might have alerted Dog (their unnamed name for Cal) and

Maurice was tired of reminding the weasel to keep them in line. He trusted his gang but only to a certain extent—especially since, given his poor eyesight, they mostly all looked the same. They all knew the story of Dog, the infamous partner-turned-traitor who abandoned the Rubbish Heap, and left the Fells in disarray. Over the past decade, history had morphed into a tall tale benefiting Maurice and intensely vilifying Cal, to the point now where the truth didn't matter, and the less detail shared, the better. Maurice was their Robin Hood. The outsider who poached from the "civilized" Woods, those who saw themselves as above the denizens of the Rubbish Heap. The maverick who stood up against the false king, the bear tyrant, watching from above. The idea of finally exacting revenge against Dog for the wrongs he'd caused stoked a fire in the gang with such vigor that Maurice had feared he might start a war. The night's visit served its purpose, and gave them something to nibble on, to take back and babble about with the rest of the crew.

Maurice had continued at a slow pace after the gang slipped away, and when certain he was alone, uncorked his bottled rage. Slamming the sack to the ground he'd chittered and chattered about, scratching at trees, savaging limbs between his teeth, until he collapsed to the dirt exhausted, bad hip throbbing with his heart beat.

"Oooo! Oooo!" he cried, sucking in air through pursed lips. "I'm too old for this."

It felt good to go wild, but he'd be sore for it in the morning. He'd told Cal the truth—his boys had spotted him acting strange, aimless, in the Fells. It could not have been a coincidence that Old Brown came down off his throne as well, and the absence of Winifred, the look in Cal's eyes when he'd mentioned the sickness, gave him more questions than he'd had before he went out. Had the two met in the Fells? Was something afoot? There was a part of him—an old grudge-bearing part—that wished he'd ordered his boys into the house and murdered Cal and his pups. But Cal deserved better—a prolonged suffering, like the one he'd brought on Maurice. Sure, there had been others there to assist him over the years. A pair of weasels. A possum he never should have trusted. And even a gutsy river otter who took an unsettling pleasure in poaching his own kind. Each had served well until greed and a lust for more power led to inevitable coup attempts. An ambush by the weasels took his right eye. A push over a (thankfully) short cliff from the possum gave him the bad hip. By the time the river otter turned, he'd learned his lesson so he knocked the otter out with a stiff drink and (for the irony) drowned him in the river. The Rubbish Heap's thick-headed vermin were too easily influenced, and after the otter stunt, which carried mandatory attendance, he vowed to take it all on himself. Thus Cal was, in the end, the source of all his past troubles. Was Winifred to be the beginning of his revenge? If she'd gotten sick . . . if she was the one who—

As tired as he was, working himself up would only do harm. Time would tell. There was work to be done, but first a gift to deliver.

Hidden deep within the Fells, the Rubbish Heap was just that—a giant mound of dead, debris, and garbage. While no record existed of its first days, it had piled up over decades like a bizarre bird's nest, tunneled out by generations of rodents, becoming a nightmarish maze. Maurice had stumbled onto it early in life, when a young raccoon's scavenging lifestyle led him on a bit of a winter wander. The inhabitants at the time were more of a collection of bickering fools than a gang, but once he moved in (fought his way in) and they (especially the weasels) quickly learned to respect his cunning and strength, they began to organize. Tunnels were enlarged to accommodate his size. Guards posted at main entrances, while others were sealed to keep out unwanted guests. The Great Scavenge began in the darkest hours of the harsh winter, Maurice leading his band to scour the Fells for the dead and dying on which they fed, smuggling bones, hide, and other items for trade across the land. Once the weak were taken, they set traps for the strong, becoming the boogie men of the Fells, cursed aloud as the *poachers*. A lost puppy became his right hand, and business was good—for a time. As the gang crossed the river into the Woods with increased frequency, they began to court trouble, venturing out with Cal one crisp fall morning to discover an entire hunting party, one-third of his gang, savaged, piled atop one another in a clearing beside the river. Old Brown had been a thorn in his side ever since, an unstoppable force of nature sending a vicious message in blood if the gang overstepped. The bear's uncanny ability to toy with him threatened to drive Maurice mad on each occasion, wondering why the self-described guardian had never come for him. But as strong as his curiosity was, Maurice had no death wish, and wasn't about to climb the mountain and ask—though once, against Cal's counsel, he'd sent a party bearing a white flag to offer a truce, and never heard from them again.

Maurice spit a series of short barks, code for his friendly arrival, as he stepped out toward the Rubbish Heap. Though most of the gang could see relatively well in the dark, late nights and early mornings were ripe for mishaps, and Maurice took it upon himself to be a good example. Seldom had a week passed without the rats accidentally cannibalizing one of their own, and while some idiocy was acceptable, security was a priority.

Four torches illuminated the main entrance, hung atop skinny tree trunks that had been felled and buried, angled out like pikes, a safe distance from the mound. Due to the inherent flammable nature of the rubbish, fire was strictly banned from the inside. The natural decaying process of the mound created its own heat, making it quite popular during the late fall and winter months, especially after the saunas opened with the first snow. Overcrowding was a yearly problem, but the visitors stuffed the gang's coffers with all manner of trade goods, and there were dependable recruits to replace those on Maurice's list.

"Like these two," Maurice said to himself as he approached the distracted guards, as non-deserving as they were of the title. When he neared the torches, his arrival startled the pair of stoats, each scrambling to his feet. The first grabbed a crude spear he'd leaned against the wall, and shouted, as he'd been instructed,

"Who goes there?" while the second, after he discovered his waist bare of weaponry, raised his claws and snarled.

"Pathetic," Maurice said as he passed between the pikes. "Who put you two on the schedule? It's me, you idiots." The pair crowded together, blocking the entrance as the empty-handed stoat shouted for him to halt. Maurice stopped less than a foot from the tip of the spear, arms out wide in disbelief. The guards stared at him, fixated on his head.

"Oh, you have got to be kidding." Maurice stepped back, grabbed the rabbit skin by the ears and pulled back and forth, yanking the mask off his head.

The stoats gasped at the revelation, falling to their knees, groveling with apologies—while simultaneously attempting to sweep their card game and acorn bets underfoot. Maurice slapped the spear-toting stoat in the face with the rabbit mask.

"Clean this up. At least *pretend* to be doing your job." Maurice glared at them as he passed, providing terse instruction to double the guard, with patrols hitting the area around the mound until sunrise.

"Why do I even bother?" Maurice whispered to himself, shaking his head. Once inside and out of sight, he finally relaxed, taking in a deep breath of humid rot-laced air. "Damn it feels good to be home." He paused to let his eyes adjust to the darkness, and entered the maze.

Maurice had committed much of the tunnels to memory, though it seemed like new alleyways of varying size appeared on a semi-regular basis. Small holes had been cut in the ceiling at most junctures to allow for fumes to escape and sunlight to enter. He clutched the bag to his chest as he made his way deeper into the center of the mound, and down, underground as the tunnel curved below, walls turning to damp earth. He'd dug many of these subterranean paths himself, and he took a sense of pride in how well and how long they'd held up. He squeezed sideways, sucking in his gut to pop through a shortcut that took him past his messy quarters. He ducked into the small room, tossed the rabbit mask onto his straw-stuffed mattress, and stepped back into the main tunnel.

"Jefferson!" he called. "Jefferson? Where are you?"

A tiny rat poked his head out of a small divot, high in the side of the tunnel wall. His left ear was marked with several holes that made it look like a piece of decayed swiss cheese. He rubbed his eyes, and looked around every which way until he at last found Maurice.

"Boss. You're back."

"Yes. You can get down now."

Jefferson peeked over the edge of the divot, and gulped as he eyed the distance to the floor. "A little help? My legs get so tired climbing up here that I worry I might fall."

Maurice let out a long sigh, his disappointment failing to register with the rat as the raccoon offered an arm to help his toady down. Jefferson's full name was Jefferson III, but it could have been IV or V as there were several Jeffersons that came before him. Maurice had become confused at one point over the course of the prior year and decided to simply call them all

79

(past, present, and future) Jefferson, in the hope of preventing any further confusion. (Though given their relatively short life expectancy, there was still an issue as to which generation he'd told what and when.)

Maurice had found it impossible to fully trust anyone in his gang after Cal abandoned him, but after years spent trapped with his own thoughts, Jefferson was his solution—a series of rats he kept isolated in the deepest parts of the Rubbish Heap, away from the conniving masses—his own personal sounding board.

"How is she doing? Has there been any progress in her condition?"

"Sleeping, mostly. As you requested, I cleaned the last of the mud and debris from her fur. She's not *exactly* what I expected her to look like."

"You've never met another raccoon besides me, Jefferson. Do all your brothers and sisters look alike?" The rat scratched at his chin, contemplating the question. "Never mind. That was a poor example. Anyway, moving on, I haven't encountered another of my kind since I was exiled to the Fells. This is a historic day, Jefferson, decades in the making. I want you to remember that."

"Yessir!" Jefferson gave his head a flick that bobbled his skull into the wall, as if the action would permanently inscribe the memory in his small brain.

A soft mewling sound echoed close by as they neared the end of the tunnel, a final elbow cutting back to their destination. Chains rattled with anticipation as they made the turn.

"Good evening my dear cousin! How are you feeling?" Maurice said, stopping in the entrance to the cel . "I didn't want to wake you, but I knew you'd be hungry."

The (slightly less) filthy creature lunged for him, claws outstretched to strike, only to be pulled down by the leather straps chained around her wrists.

"I know," Maurice said, noting the restraints. "I don't like them either but it's for both our protection. I'll remove them as soon as you're better—any day now."

He forced a smile. The situation wasn't promising but he was still hopeful. He had discovered the sickly striped animal unconscious in the Fells two nights prior, half covered in mud, and determined it to be his cousin Clem (short for Clementine) who he hadn't seen since they were mere babies. In fact, it had been so long that he wasn't certain it was Clem, and not having uttered more than a growl, hiss, and a purr since waking, he hadn't been able to confirm. But now seeing her mostly clean, he *knew* it had to be her, and his heart fluttered at the sight of true family after all these years. Maurice had felt betrayed when Cal left him behind for Winifred, but even more so, he felt a sense of envy that burned deep inside his heart at his inability to replicate the same sense of family. His idea of family—him and Cal—was proven false when Cal came to him awestruck by another dog, and in that moment Maurice knew nothing but his own kind would do.

Like fire, the very ill were banned from the Rubbish Heap, and he'd broken his own rules, sneaking her inside under an old blood-stained sheet as a catch (Beaver? Otter? He'd fumbled on the spot in front of the guards.) that he intended to handle himself, dragging her to the only place he could think of, an old unused cell near his own hole. Whatever illness possessed her had turned her savage and if it wasn't for his quick thinking, and presence when she woke, he might be dead, or wearing patches over both eyes, and surely dead soon after.

Jefferson tugged on a bit of Maurice's fur to get his attention. "What is it?"

"I noticed a deep bite mark on her left leg when I was cleaning her up. Looks as if it hasn't healed well."

Maurice crouched down beside Jefferson. "Are you a doctor, Jefferson?"

"No-no, sir."

"And what did we discuss?"

"Nothing is to leave this room. Clem is going to get better and join the ranks of the Rubbish Heap gang. Then we can tell others what happened and what a great job I did."

"No, we can never tell anyone what happened down here."

"Yes, I mean, n-no," Jefferson stammered.

"Good. Thank you for your observation."

Maurice made a mental note to have Jefferson replaced when Clem was past the affliction and back on her feet. Once sick, always sick. As Maurice knew all too well, no one else could know of her condition. It had been nearly two decades since he was banished from the Woods to the Fells after one of his neighbors had outed him as shut-in with fever for days. He'd been too weak to fight it and awoke one morning face down on the other side of the river, his left shoulder blade seared with a brand—a snake in the shape of an S. Against Mother Nature's wishes, he'd recovered and sought refuge in the Rubbish Heap. But even they, vermin of the lowest ilk, wanted no part of him after catching sight of his brand. If he hadn't lost control in the moment and throttled their leader at the time (a sharp-tongued coward of a weasel) he would have been left to wander as an outcast, eventually ridden down by those fearing what he might carry.

Maurice dug into his sack, pulled out the head, and gently tossed it across the room. Clem had rejected the garbage Maurice had brought the past two nights, and his chancing upon rabbit was a good opportunity to try something new.

"Did Winifred bite you? A dog. Floppy ears." Maurice mimed floppy ears and an elongated face with his paws, imitating a woof for good measure. Clem looked up from her meal, staring at him. "Is that why you are sick? No? You don't know?

"Leave me all those years ago only to send your wife back with bark and bite and take everything again, huh? Fitting." He took a step forward and she leapt at him, biting at the air, the restraints holding back her claws. Jefferson squeaked and hurried behind Maurice for protection.

Maurice apologized as he retreated to the entrance, nearly tripping over Jefferson. "I'd be upset if someone interrupted my dinner, too. We'll try again after you've had your fill and gotten some rest." He turned and tossed Jefferson ahead of him, out of the way in frustration, then bowed his goodbye and ducked out into the tunnel.

Clem hissed, lunged for him again as he departed, her taut limbs straining against the chains. Her feet slid backward in the soil until her left foot caught on an exposed root. She kicked out, a burst of earth showering her back, left arm suddenly free. She smiled, examining the result. Quite pleased, she batted the savaged head into the corner, pulled her meal up onto her lap, and ate.

PART 2

THE

WILD

WOOD

5

After Maurice skulked away, Cal had remained vigilant on the porch, waiting for the raccoon and his cronies to double-back to try to catch him off-guard. The longer he waited, the more his eyes played tricks on him, turning shadows and wind-blown trees into momentary threats that spiked his adrenaline. When his eyelids began to droop he called it quits and turned in, adding a pair of logs to the fire before snuggling up to the boys. Gus had followed his father's instruction and gone back to sleep. However, rest remained elusive for Cal. Every minute he spent with his eyes closed was matched with another wide awake, his ears alerting him to a creak or crack, the cry of a distant bird, or simply another gust of wind. His paranoia got the best of him, and not for a minute did he feel safe. If not for his desire to comfort his boys, he would have spent the rest of the night pacing the cabin, bracing for the worst. At half-past dawn the boys stirred him awake, their stomachs rumbling with hunger. While they dressed for school, Cal brewed coffee and prepped breakfast—stale bread with the remnants of a jar of gooseberry preserves. Perhaps because they were running late, or they could read the intense fatigue in Cal's face, the boys left matters concerning their mother lie, and after dressing in button-down plaid shirts (Franklin in yellow with green stripes, Gus in blue with red stripes), they focused on devouring their two slices each.

Cal stepped outside with a mug of dark coffee in each paw, letting the screen door slap shut behind him.

"Easy." Billiam grimaced at the loud sound, massaging his right temple. He stood off to the side of the porch in the grass, clear of the path muddied by the rain, a package tucked under his left arm. The morning sun broke through the clouds as Cal approached, causing him to squint.

"Sorry, couldn't sleep last night" Cal said, handing the badger a mug. Billiam thanked him, blowing across the rim of the mug before taking a small sip.

"Blech. You put sugar in this, didn't you?"

"Always."

"*Always*? Since when is *always*?"

Cal shrugged, took a gulp from his mug.

"Right, next time I'll bring a thermos." Billiam crouched down, dipped a claw into the damp earth, and pinched a thimble full of dirt. He rubbed his fingers together, sprinkling granules of dirt over his coffee.

Cal raised an eyebrow. "Really?"

"You got a better idea? It's fine. I do it all the time. Nothing like a little bitter earth with my bitter coffee to ease my bitter soul. Look," he said, taking a long sip, smacking his tongue against the roof of his mouth. "Delicious."

"I could . . . make more, you know."

"No time for that. Besides—well, look at that." Billiam crouched back down. In the spot he previously scraped wriggled a fat earth-worm. "Coming out for the rain, were you?" He plucked the worm, and feinted a throw at Cal, causing him to back him up, before slipping the morsel into his coffee.

"Now I've seen everything," Cal said.

"What? Never tried a worm, have you? If this shortage keeps for much longer, they'll be top of the menu at the badger house. We'll have you over. I'll teach you the family recipe."

"You're taking that home with you."

"Good, I'll need a warm up."

Billiam snuck a glance at his wristwatch, near spilling some of his coffee in the process. "What are they doing in there?"

"The boys are finishing up their breakfast. I'm letting them take their time. I'm the reason we're late after all—they had to wake me up."

"Any word from Winifred?"

Cal licked his lips, took a deep pull from his coffee, the hot liquid singeing his throat, but he kept at it, filling the silence. He brought the mug down empty, shook his head.

"Say no more." Billiam thrust the package he'd been holding at Cal, forced him to take it with his free paw. "I know you're never one to ask for help, so just accept the gift. I put it together last night—an extra loaf of rye, root vegetables and a few salted fish."

Cal examined the package, shaking his head. "I can't accept this."

"Yes, you can and will. One, I'm a hoarder. The cellar is overloaded with this and that, and if I don't clean up my act, the missus has threatened to toss the good stuff. Two, as the Woods' sole elected official, it's my duty to look after my constituents. It's not much, but it will keep your mind off food for a few days, which should be enough to keep you from eating a neighbor, or whatever other activity you may have done, or may not be doing, or plan on completing. Three, you're a great friend, Cal, and it hurts to see you this way. Four—"

Cal tucked the package under his arm, reached out and squeezed Billiam's shoulder. "Thank you," he said. "This is very kind. Please pass on my thanks to the family."

Cal tilted his mug and poured out the dregs. "I'll take this in and shoo them out."

"Billiam Junior, let's go!" the badger called as Cal hit the steps, headed inside.

A moment later Billy and Gus spilled from the house and bounced across the porch, blurting short, required apologies. Franklin caught the door from closing behind them. Sullen and moody, he brushed past Billiam, and took off at a slow pace, mumbling grievances against his annoying brother and his friend. The two quickly caught up, prodding Franklin by slapping at his tail before sprinting off to play their own games, chasing each other back and forth across the path.

"Stay out of the mud!" Billiam reminded his son, who

promptly ignored him as he promptly slid through a slick patch. The young badger flirted with losing his balance as he reached out to tag Gus, who let out a whoop as he managed to avoid the tag and stay upright, his rubber boots adding a little squeak to each step. Billiam took a handkerchief from his breast pocket and slapped it against his forehead. "The sun is barely up and my kid is giving me nervous sweats. I spent ten minutes picking out dirt between his toes and scraping his nails before the missus would let us in last night."

"If a little mud is your main worry, I think you're doing just fine."

"Tell me about it. We pull the Moon Festival off and maybe I'll finally sleep—if the twins let me."

Cal forced a smile as they continued after the kids, wishing he'd brought more coffee, at least something to keep his hands occupied and break up the conversation. Billiam was a talker, and up until then Cal had used the conversation to keep his mind of his troubles, but as they left the cabin he couldn't help but notice the slew of tracks in addition to the fresh badger and dog prints. Maurice's prints were easy to spot with his limp, the others, perhaps a dozen or more, were impossible to identify without close examination. Thankfully Billiam was oblivious, too lost in conversation with himself to notice. Likewise, the boys and their games. If it got out that Cal had been in the Fells and that Maurice had paid him a visit the very same night . . .

How do you think it would look, you dumb mutt?

Outside of his clashes with Old Brown, Cal had never been fully identified as the dog running with the Rubbish Heap gang, but there had been enough rumor to peg him as guilty— *a poacher*. He'd maintained cover stories—a half-brother he'd worked for, logging at Basin Lake—and took long winding routes to the Fells, taking time to cover his tracks. Still, parents hid their children around him. Duchess preferred he do his shopping at the General Store late at night, after hours. Even those few who interacted with him at the most basic level, Billiam included, would only do so out of sight and earshot of others. How he had wanted to leave the world behind and settle in the home he'd worked so hard to afford, but he lacked the courage to face the consequences. It took Winifred's arrival to finally turn him away, a chance fire to win over most of the inhabitants. It could all be so easily undone. He still caught a glimpse of his former life in the eyes of the elderly, those who had fought for what they had, who cursed him as a traitor under their breath, to which side it didn't matter. To have one turn in his past left the possibility for another. He'd always be a wolf among them.

* * *

From the western edge of the Woods, the dogs and badgers had one of the longest commutes to school each day, which still wasn't very far. Cal considered the walk to be a warm-up for the day, a good stretching of the legs that got his mind working and prevented him from plopping back into bed. They always left early enough, even when running late, to ensure the kids would run across their friends on the way and have time to mingle before Nutbrown's customary crackdown. The old squirrel ran a tight schedule, and any behavior deemed out of line was met with a swift rap on the knuckles with her pint-sized ruler. Franklin and Gus had both been on the receiving end multiple times—"They're puppies," Cal had explained to her in their defense. "What do you expect?"—and used their time outside to burn off as much energy as possible before gluing themselves to their seats.

As they neared the more populated center of the Woods, the kids, even Franklin, ran up ahead to greet their friends.

Pigs: Ted sporting his two-sizes-too-small pork pie hat, and his wife Helen with their son, Jeffrey. The little rotund piglet was covered with mud from the waist down, per usual. He was nice enough, but somehow managed to hunt down and roll in the stuff during even the driest of months—an ability his parents were immeasurably proud of.

Otters: Hugo and Mol, straying from their small home along the river to deliver their daughter, Cate, who wore a pink bow around her neck. She'd often be excused during lunch break to take a dip in the river. Much like piglets and mud, young otters possessed a penchant for becoming intensely irritable when dried out.

Tortoises from the south bog: Hank, absent his wife, Myrtle, with his son, Clayton. It was an old wives' tale that marked the species as slow, though Gus relayed stories of Clayton using it to his advantage to prod their teacher. For example, moving painfully slow to deliver paperwork to her desk while the class tried to hide their laughter and Nutbrown fumed, eventually snatching the work from him herself to end the charade.

Half-blind opossums: Jarvis and Robin, clutching their son Roy, navigating the trees and pitfalls as a family. Jarvis kept his eyes on the ground, Robin's stayed straight ahead, while Roy focused on listening to the sounds around them. This always seemed exhausting to Cal, but he quietly cheered them for their determination to have their son fit in with others during the daylight hours.

The young rabbit family of four was absent, much to Cal's relief. Franklin was old enough to know better, but he couldn't be certain Gus wouldn't run up to them and exclaim, with innocent enthusiasm, "Guess what we ate for dinner last night?" and proceed to explain the contents of the stew.

And then there were beavers and other small folk, and many deer. Cal and Billiam fell in with the pack and offered morning greetings. "Tommy," Billiam said, waving to a large six-point buck.

"It's Arnold," the deer scoffed, puffing out his chest. Billiam shrugged, waving off the mistake.

"I can never tell them apart," Billiam confessed to Cal. "At a planning meeting last week, Jeanie told me to count the spots on her leg if I needed help identifying her at the Moon Festival. So, I'm supposed to be some creeper staring at her legs? There are *eight* spots, and they're not all grouped together. Plus, with all these thoughts swirling in my head, I have to count out loud or I lose track of the numbers."

"Sounds embarrassing," Cal said.

"You think? Sheesh. Can't please these guys."

"I can hear you," Arnold said, turning to the group of deer beside him. "*These* guys."

"See what I mean?" Billiam rolled his eyes. "I'm trying to have a private conversation and they butt their way right in."

"You want to say that to my face, badger?"

Billiam scurried around Cal, putting his friend between him and the buck. "It's Billiam to you, deer."

Arnold pranced over, threatening to shoulder Cal out of the way. "You want to go right now, badger? Make a scene in front of the kids? Give them something to talk about all day while they're bored? Might as well get my money's worth. What do we pay you for, anyway?"

"I'm *the* elected official of the Woods and I will not tolerate such treatment. You better—"

Cal spread his arms out wide to create a buffer between the two as they jawed at each other. "Let's keep it civil. Once the kids are off we can hash this out over breakfast as adults."

"I'm not *hungry*," Arnold said. "Don't you sense the chill in the air? Winter will be upon us soon. This is not the time for spring tea or summer brunch."

"Okay, over coffee then."

"I've already *had* my fill," Billiam said. "Why don't we pick a tree out to huddle around on the way back? We can patch things up and Arnold can lose the attitude and chew some bark. Maybe a maple?" Then on the side to Cal he whispered, "Is there sap in the bark?"

"Is that supposed to be a joke, badger? Do you think we enjoy stripping trees to fill our starving bellies in the dead of winter? Would you feed your family bowls of frosted dirt?"

"Well, actually," Billiam began, until Cal cuffed him in the shoulder, cutting him off. Cal could tell he was thinking of the pinch of earth he'd added to his mug. The longer the back and forth continued between the two stubborn animals, the more heated it would get, and he had no desire to stand between the two—or as it was more likely, hold back Arnold while Billiam fled as fast as his legs could carry him.

The pair was about to continue when a sharp whistle cut the air, snatching their attention. In a small clearing a hundred yards ahead of them, past a trickle of a creek, stood the one-room school house. It had been rebuilt with brick after the fire, red with white trim, gray shingles for the roof and a small overhang above the entrance. A large window on each side of the front door, and three windows along each side of the building let in plenty of natural light. A small chimney poked through the roof emitting a wisp of wood smoke. The door was open, and the young were saying their farewells to their parents and beginning to file in. Cal, Billiam, and Arnold had fallen behind the pack amid their bickering. Gus waved to his father as he followed his brother inside. He sported an anxious frown, like he was doing his best to hold back tears.

The moment jarred Cal and tore at his heart, a sudden reminder of his world crashing down around him. He wanted nothing but to sprint to Gus's side, to pull him tight against his chest and comfort him. But before Cal could perform more than a half-wave and take two steps, Gus was inside. To follow would only make things worse, adding the embarrassment of Nutbrown threatening Cal with her ruler to get out, as parents were not allowed inside.

Beside the door, atop a wooden stool of medium height, stood Sir George Washington, a most regal toad, clad in thick winter parka with hood drawn tight over his head, antique harpoon gun slung over his shoulder. The proud guard glared at the trio, gave a second short whistle, and drew a webbed digit across his neck, ordering them to cut it out.

"Look what you've done, badger. Now the toad's all riled up," Arnold said.

"Me? You're the one who sticks out with your melodramatic snorts and sighs. Bet my whiskers you get reprimanded first."

"Not today," Arnold countered. "It's been a while since I've witnessed rent-a-guard exercise his power. I think we're all in for a lecture."

At least that's something you two are close to agreeing on, thought Cal as they approached the school. The toad hopped down from his perch as they neared, harpoons jangling loose in a pouch on his back.

"G'morning fellas," GW said with a slight tip of his head. "What's the ruckus all about? I'm supposed to be on lookout for the kids but all I see is the three of you causing a scene on a nice school morning."

"I didn't know it was going to snow today," Arnold said, chuckling at his own joke. "Good to know you won't be abandoning your post to warm up." Arnold finished with an awkward salute, mocking the toad.

"Very funny—and offensive to veterans on several levels. Stay after drop-off and I'll skin one of those legs. Give me a nice scarf and you a taste of the cool autumn breeze."

"I'll pass. My kids get all the protection they need from me, thank you. If our deer rules applied, I'd challenge you and send you packing back to the bog where you belong."

"Try me, Arnold. There are worse things out there than you."

Cal moved to calm the tension. Billiam stuck an arm out, holding him back, and gave him a wink. The badger cleared his throat.

"Gentlemen, I think we can all agree with our most regal friend here that this is indeed a crisp, beautiful morning, and we should be doing our best to enjoy these last days before the winter snow." GW folded his arms over his chest, and Arnold rolled his eyes, mumbled, "I'm not sitting through this," and began to walk away as Billiam continued. "And as the Woods' sole elected official I want to thank you for standing watch over our children. It's been a wonderful gesture, your volunteering your time over the last two years since your return. But . . . this is all a little much, don't you think?"

"A little much?" asked GW. "What's a little much?"

"You know, the whistling and the harpoons jangling about. How old is that gun anyway?"

"It belonged to my uncle."

"Right. It's a little much, no?"

"Please excuse us, we need to have a word." Cal took Billiam by the arm and dragged him, kicking, around the side of the school.

"Ow, you're pinching a nerve!" Billiam hissed.

"What the hell are you doing?"

Billiam brushed the sleeve of his suit coat. "I don't like his tone."

"His *tone*? That toad will stand outside that door in a *blizzard*. He volunteers his time. You remember the fire. What's wrong with a little reassurance?"

"From a toad."

The pair both suddenly felt as if they were being watched, turned back to the school to see the children looking at them, Nutbrown standing at the closest window, all the anger a squirrel could muster channeled into her face. When she had their attention, she bit at the air, jumped up onto the nearest desk, bounding to the top of the window where she latched onto a hook and descended with the shade, hiding them from view. The pair paused for a moment, processing the interaction.

"A veteran toad," Cal continued. "You should apologize."

"Never."

"Fine, I'll apologize for you."

Billiam kicked a clod of dirt. "Is this all really necessary?" he asked. Cal ignored him and rounded the corner to the front of the school. He apologized to GW, though the toad shook his head and dismissed the act as unnecessary.

"I appreciate your support but spare me your sympathy. A soldier must be able to withstand harsh criticism in the face of his duty. No matter the insults, I'll continue to keep watch while your children are within these walls."

Cal thanked him and left, heading north toward the river. When he reached the edge of the clearing, Billiam crept around the back of the school and called out to him.

"Hey, wait up! You want to check out the setup for the Moon Festival? It's going to be a good one this year. Brings back a lot of memories."

"Memories . . ." thought Cal. He'd done enough reminiscing on his own. Cal politely declined, telling his friend he was busy, and jogged past the alarm bell and off through the trees. Billiam picked up a thin stick and threw it toward the bell, but its odd shape sent it spiraling to the ground only a few feet away.

After the fire that consumed the old schoolhouse and the surrounding Woods, several bells were hung atop posts scattered throughout the area—one by the school, a second near the center of the Woods, close to the General Store, and a third on the bridge to the east—in the hope of quickly alerting the community in case of an emergency.

Billiam had helped install them after the fire, but other than kids playing false alarms in the immediate aftermath, he couldn't recall a time when they'd been put to use. Which was a good thing, but it only increased his level of general unease at the sight of them.

The badger watched his friend go. He wandered aimlessly around the clearing, staring at the ground, contemplating life, the morning, his under-appreciated role in the community. Feeling sorry for himself, he looked up to see Nutbrown again, drawing her ruler back and forth across the glass, huffing with rage. She pointed at him, and Billiam looked around, pointing at himself as if there could be any question who she was targeting. He ran from the clearing, eager to escape the threat of her wrath.

6

The class knew better than to laugh when Nutbrown pressed her nose against the window and pounded on the glass to scare off the distraction outside. Gus looked back over his shoulder at the clock mounted on the wall beside the door (one minute past was a late start—they were going on three) and hoped it wasn't his father again. Jeffrey had chuckled when Gus's father and Mr. Billiam had interrupted the first minutes of the day, his piggy snort drawing the ire of their instructor. With an oversized pencil, Nutbrown scrawled on a piece of paper on her desk. The entire class knew it was the young pig's name, and what it meant (it wasn't good), and Jeffrey covered his mouth and snout to muffle a squeal. Billy, to Gus's left, had leaned over and whispered, "That's what you get!" but when the second disruption turned out to be his father alone, he made himself small, put his head down and doodled trees in the margins of his workbook. Drawing a variety of deciduous trees in books became a coping mechanism for Billy that day, something he'd eventually catch hell for, but by the time Nutbrown discovered his habit, he'd get close to a year of practice under his belt and become rather impressive. Nutbrown would still give him a few raps and confiscate his books to maintain her image, but later, after the other children had left, she'd surprise him by giving his books back and insisting he nurture his gift under the study of Rogers, a mole, a painter, and a hermit famous for his depictions of the fall.

Seating in the classroom was assigned by age, with the youngest in the front row. Gus enjoyed his seat near the middle of the room, and Franklin even more so in the back. Nutbrown was a strong proponent of the power of failure as the best way to learn, and when forced to call on a student for an answer, began with the front before working her way back, ensuring the maximum number of embarrassing mumbles and stumbles. Although the young dealt with the stress of being put on the spot, they also sat closest to the small hearth, a blessing during the cold winter months when Franklin and some of the older kids in the back spent much of the day wrapped in layers. After the old school burned down, Nutbrown pledged to never light a fire the size of which might endanger the children. Better to be cold and safe. On this occasion, their instructor had lit a small fire to take the morning chill off, cedar logs giving the school a pleasant aroma.

While Nutbrown was still dealing with the distraction at the window, Gus felt a poke in his lower back. He continued to face forward, doing his best to ignore the prodding from Beatrix, his daily nemesis since returning from summer break. As if giving him warning, each time she adjusted herself in her seat, her beaver tail slapped against the back of her chair before she stretched forward under her desk with a pencil. When he'd first complained at home, his mother had responded with the theory that she probably liked Gus, and seeking his attention was her way of showing it. But Gus found it annoying at best—worst when she teased him with bitter gossip, trying to drag him down to her level and make him miserable, too (or at least that's what Franklin had told him she was doing).

"Psst!" she whispered. When he didn't acknowledge her, she poked him again, and then again, this time with enough force to sting.

"Stop it!" he whispered, cocking his head to the side to look back at her. "What do you want?"

"I heard your mom is sick."

Gus eyed her for a moment, trying to gauge her expression. Did she know something about his mother?

"It's bad," she said. "Isn't it? That's what I heard anyway."

He twisted slightly to get a better look and she shrank back from over her desk, a nervous grin on her face, big buck teeth pressing into her bottom lip. No, he decided, turning back around, she knew nothing. That didn't stop her from giving him another jab, but by then Nutbrown had run off Mr. Billiam and returned her attention to the class, silencing Beatrix's game.

"Please remind your parents that drop-off is to be just that, a *drop-off*. It is imperative that we begin class promptly each and every day to ensure your maximum learning potential."

Nutbrown paced in front of her desk as she spoke and adjusted the sleeves of her outfit, a long olive-colored dress with puffy shoulders and frills around her waist. After a brief lecture on school procedures, the importance of communication and the responsibilities of being an active student in her class, Nutbrown snatched a thin piece of chalk from a dish and began the first lesson, as she did daily, with mathematics.

Much of the class shifted in their small desks, noisily assembling papers and pencils as a passive protest, fearful of what reprisal an audible groan might bring. But Gus loved math and looked forward to the creative word problems Nutbrown tapped out on the blackboard. It wasn't easy for him, but it always had been for Franklin, and his older brother had made a point (though more reluctantly as they grew older) to tutor Gus whenever he had trouble with his homework. Gus liked Nutbrown, too. His father had said her ball of twine was wound too tight (whatever that meant), but Gus loved to learn and each day brought something new. His mother had helped him recognize that the squirrel's tough love was a good thing that kept his brother and him in line. If anything, it pressured him to focus and get his work done so he could go outside and play— which, at the end of the day, is all a pup wants to do.

With her back to the class, Nutbrown spoke aloud as she wrote the first problem on the board. Gus listened intently, writing along with her. He'd taken his squeaky boots off and placed them beside the door when he'd come in. It felt good to tap his feet against the wood floor.

The problem was unusually long—multiple paragraphs in length about two foxes skipping stones on a lake—to begin class. Gus's mind began to drift as he copied the words down. Each summer their mother would take Franklin and him on long walks south to Baba Pond on the edge of the bog. They'd collect rocks of all shapes and sizes on the way, as many as their little paws could carry (or hand off to their mother). At the pond they'd split a bag of hard licorice sweets, and take turns skipping the rocks across the calm water. The longer Nutbrown wrote, the clearer the memories became and Gus found himself taken by a profound sense of sadness. A tear escaped down his cheek as his eyes began to water and before long, he was crying, his face buried in his arms on his desk, his body wracked with sobs. For the first time in memory, he questioned his father's word—what if everything *wasn't* okay—and his sense of hope flickered. If he could see her, hear her voice, if only for a moment . . .

He felt a poke on his back, then another, closer to his spine.

"Psst! Why are you crying?" Beatrix asked. When he didn't acknowledge her, she prodded him again. "Are you upset about your mother? I know what it's—"

Gus spun around to confront her. "Stop it! Just stop it!" he shouted. Beatrix shrank back in her chair, her face shading beet red as her eyes flitted between Gus and the classmates surrounding them who'd all turned their attention to the pair.

"Gus! What is the meaning of this outburst?" Nutbrown screeched from her position at the blackboard. It was only then that Gus realized what he'd done, slowly turning back around to receive his fate.

"Well? Speak up now. We've had enough interruptions this morning for this to drag on any longer."

"She won't stop poking me in the back," Gus said, wiping away his tears.

"Is this true, Beatrix? You look guilty enough," Nutbrown said, placing her chalk back in the dish, rubbing the dust from her paws against her dress. Beatrix shook her head no, but her participation read obvious on her face. "Either way, seems hardly worth the outburst. Are you in pain? Why are you crying?"

Gus stared at his desk, sniffling, wishing he had a handkerchief to wipe his nose. He felt the sadness growing in his heart with each tick of the clock. He needed to say something—*anything*—but he knew the second he opened his mouth he'd be a bawling mess.

"Out with it now." Nutbrown clapped her paws together, sending a small puff of chalk dust into the air. "You're only making things worse."

"He's being a baby," Beatrix said, barely more than a whisper.

"What was that?" Nutbrown stepped forward into the front row to better listen.

"You shut your mouth," Franklin snapped, jaw clenched, staring down the beaver, who looked back wide-eyed in terror. The entire class shifted their attention to the older dog, gasping at the audacity.

"Franklin!" Nutbrown pressed a paw over her chest in shock.

Beatrix's horror morphed into a crooked smile, and she spoke up again, louder this time. "His mom is sick and he's being a baby."

"Just because you don't have a mom doesn't mean you need to pick on Gus," Franklin said.

Jaws dropped around the room. It was well known that Beatrix's mother had died carrying a sibling before Beatrix was even a year old. No one talked about it, and sometimes Gus wondered if this is why she seemed miserable.

Beatrix began to cry. Nutbrown screamed for order, clenching her paws as if expecting to have her notorious ruler in hand, and when she found nothing, she spun to her desk, and rummaged through papers to hunt for it.

Franklin stood and threw his pack over a shoulder. He appeared so cool and collected amid the chaos, but Gus could see through the facade in his eyes—he was barely holding it together, playing tough to cover the wave of emotion on the verge of crashing down.

"Let's go, Gus," Franklin said, heading for the door. "We're getting out of here."

Gus didn't hesitate—stuffed his things back into his bag, and hurried after his older brother, ignoring Beatrix's sobs as he ran to the back.

"Where do you think *you're* going?" Nutbrown stalked around her desk, ruler clutched so tightly in her right paw her arm shook. "You two get back here this instant!"

Gus glanced back at their teacher—he'd never seen such rage—but Franklin grabbed him by the collar, turned him back, and pushed him outside. He slammed the door without a word after they were both out.

"You are in the deepest trouble, boys!" Nutbrown railed from inside. "You and your parents better show up this evening, *or else!* "

"Come on!" Franklin said, ushering his brother into a sprint. "Don't look back."

"Too late," Gus said, blinking away tears. The image of Nutbrown banging on the window, fading away as her breath fogged the pane, was the stuff of nightmares. No wonder Mr. Billiam ran off as quickly as he did. Gus looked to Franklin as he ran, the tears running freely down his brother's tough features. A whirlwind of exhilaration flowed through Gus, from his brain to his heart, out along his limbs, tickling his ears. He found himself smiling, laughing at the absurdity of it all. Franklin returned the grin, chuckled as he grabbed Gus's paw, pulling him along, faster and faster. Together they crossed the field and disappeared into the woods.

* * *

GW slowly rocked on his stool, eyes half-shut, humming an old melancholic tune that helped him pass the time. Even though he'd caught flak from several parents for his winter gear, he tried his best to stay positive. If they knew how warm and toasty he was, they wouldn't come at him like that. His days were too long, job too important to worry about the words of others. No sir, he would not take those bitter words to heart. He watched the badger leave and spit a tiny wad of phlegm into the dirt. *No sir.*

A flock of geese flew below the gray clouds overhead, squawking, their V-shape pointed directly south past the nearby alarm bell, its weathered handle swaying quietly in the breeze. It had been a difficult morning to focus and find peace. He'd heard the growing outrage inside the school, but had become accustomed to Nutbrown's style and didn't think much of it. At times he felt sorry for the kids—on a regular basis one or another seemed to be getting into trouble, used as an example in front of the class. It had crossed his mind several times that they could have used someone like Nutbrown down in the mangroves, though he wasn't sure a bunch of green, rowdy amphibians would have taken well to an old squirrel's demands.

When the door unexpectedly burst open, GW was already off balance, and when the door unexpectedly burst open, he was so startled he fell off his stool. His stumble became a slight roll into a crouched position, his harpoon gun unslung and clutched in his hands. The harpoons had fallen out of his quiver, scattered across the grass. He kept his eyes up as he ran a webbed hand across the ground until he found the stray ammunition, which he slipped back into the quiver instead of loading into the gun. Cal's pups sprinted north away from the school. Neither had paid him any attention when they crashed outside, and he doubted they'd pay him any mind if he were to call after them. He liked the pups—good kids who said goodbye to him after school and for the most part stayed out of trouble.

GW collected the remaining harpoons from the ground and slotted the last into his weapon with a *ka-chunk*. He gave a light knock on the door to the school room, turned the knob, and headed inside.

7

Cal crouched down beside the river, his feet sinking into the muddy sediment as the current lapped against his ankles. He dipped his paws into the cold water and cupped a small, refreshing sip to his mouth. The temperature had steadily fallen since he left the school, and he longed to be home beside a warm fire. But there were still too many unanswered questions, and part of him, the long-buried savage of his youth, couldn't let Maurice's challenge go unanswered.

After having sprinted away from Billiam, Cal took his time making his way north. He stayed off trails, picking his way through the Woods. The impression of a casual stroll gave him an alibi, plus opportunity to ensure that the badger hadn't followed, and if he did run across anyone else on the way, he would be ready. Like when he sensed the young rabbit parents, Steve and Meryl, who seemed to hike parallel to him, for too long. Steve with a wicker basket in hand, Meryl with a pruning knife, trimming fungi from the base of trees. After they exchanged waves from a distance, and he imagined them hopping out of their skins, a wide shroom cap under each arm, and straight into a kettle of thick, bubbling stew: a sick joke that made his stomach rumble. It didn't help that the pigs lived close by, warm scents of yeast and spices wafting from their hovel, carried by the breeze into Cal's nose. Despite their often crusty, thrown-together appearance, the pigs were some of the best cooks in the Woods, preparing much of the food for the Moon Festival each year. Eventually, after some discussion regarding the lack of fungi variety and if they'd taken too much, the rabbits peeled off to the west and Cal sped up, only pausing once more against a tree to catch his breath and check his surroundings before heading to the river.

A good-sized log floated downstream; one of its branches extended out of the water reflecting a dusting of icy snow. Given the quickness with which it traveled, Cal half-expected the log to be pushed by a river dweller—an otter or a beaver, most likely— but as it passed he spotted neither. While he possessed no desire for company, he couldn't help feel a twinge of loneliness after not even an air bubble rose to the surface. No creatures hugged the bottom, milking the last whispers of warm fall afternoons. Only the soft drift of the log in search of a new home.

Cal chose a spot a good distance upstream from the elbow to wait with the idea to avoid an unwanted interaction with Gil. Given the events of the previous night, he wasn't sure if the catfish would ever speak to him again, and he couldn't spare the time to make things right—an undertaking which would result in Cal listening to Gil vent for hours on the lack of respect given to him (and all fish, for that matter) until he inevitably felt better, thanked Cal for his patience, and threatened him with some outlandish punishment if he told anyone of his complaints. Cal remained at the river for a moment listening, separating the wind against the trees, the distant cackle of a crow, and his own breathing from the potential echoed snap of a dry twig or crunch of dead leaves underfoot. Nothing moved within earshot; the late fall day as quiet as mid-winter.

There were three points to traverse the river near the Woods (if he didn't count holding his coat overhead and wading across, in which case nearly the entire length was accessible). Upstream from Cal, the river hugged the base of the mountain. East of Old Brown's domain, where the river turned north, three boulders spread across its width marking the end of a series of rapids. It was an easy crossing—four jumps and you were safe on the other side. The boulders were evenly spaced as if purposely arranged by hand, and even when damp, provided enough grip to prevent worry. It was a crossing Cal often used when he was working with Maurice, but for now it was too far out of the way, and would leave Cal to double back along the riverbank. The second crossing, downstream toward the bog, was a rickety bridge built just wide enough for a trader's wagon to squeeze through. The bridge held up well despite rumors that it was senior to Old Brown, having outlasted its original builders and passed annual proddings by a team of beavers, who, despite their assurances, chose to swim across rather than set foot on the structure. The creaks and cracks didn't deter Cal, but there were too many eyes on the bridge even if it was the easiest option, and he'd made too much of an effort to hide himself to be seen.

Unless he wanted to tempt hypothermia (and he most certainly *did not*), the only option left was a fallen oak tree. The thick trunk had been in place for years, appearing to have been uprooted by a storm and fallen perfectly across. In reality, rumor was the tree had been felled hundreds of yards away, but some enterprising folk had worked together to drag it through the woods, trimming the branches to provide grips—three on the left, four on the right—to pass between as one crossed. It had been propped up on each end with rocks and debris to allow for small boats to pass underneath (with passengers laying flat), though moisture still found its way, and the length of the route was slick with moss. Worst case in the summer, a slip got you a little wet. In the winter, when the river was crusted with ice, it made Cal nervous to cross, nervous enough to avoid it entirely with the pups when rumors surfaced of Woods folk crashing through the surface and drowning, trapped beneath, carried downstream, never to be seen again. But he didn't have the time to spare, so looking around again to ensure the coast was clear, Cal stepped—lightly—up to the challenge, shuffling his feet, moving from branch to branch while keeping his eyes forward, never on the water, and made it across.

* * *

Snow flurries began to fall as he made his way deep into the Fells. Trees helped to guide him over steep embankments and hurdle sharp rocks. He had to stop and look to be certain of the change, his paws stuffed inside his coat to keep them warm. Too cold for the late fall, he thought. He closed his eyes and stuck out his tongue to catch a flurry, mimicking Gus's ritual with each snow.

To Cal, the Fells had always felt like a place out of time—wild and unkempt. Fallen trees lay haphazardly across old trails, left to rot for eternity. Living trees took on a half-dead gray tone, so densely packed together, fighting for sunlight, that their limbs didn't sprout until thirty feet up the trunk, and even then they were spindly things, like spokes on a wagon wheel. The evergreens in the Fells were always the most shocking in comparison with those in the Woods. The evergreen trees in the Woods grew thick like gigantic bushes full of sticky sap. In contrast, those in the Fells were frail cousins with long, hair-like needles and narrow pinecones that spilled each fall, coating the floor. In the spring, fields of these evergreens would sprout like sickly ferns, fighting one another for nutrients in the rocky soil.

Cal heard a cry overhead and opened his eyes, startled to catch a glimpse of a broad-winged hawk circling nearby, its head cocked to the side, one eye on the ground. Cal quickly glanced at his surroundings—all naked trees and decaying leaves. Nothing thick enough to hide behind, or layered to burrow under. Then, up ahead he spotted a squat cluster of evergreens, improbably punching out from the base of a short cliff. Beside them, a large oak had fallen, uprooting its base of dirt and roots and creating a narrow tunnel between it, the evergreens, and the cliff face. Cal ducked to stay low and ran forward, hoping his timing was good as he slid over a floor of pine needles and took cover underneath the evergreens. He looked up through the branches and tried to get a bead on the hawk, but the view was obscured. He'd have to expose himself to the sky to see. His mouth ran dry. *Trapped.*

Back in his early days with the Rubbish Heap, it had been Cal's idea to work with hawks to locate animals who had fallen into their traps. It took training and near-constant bribery, but it worked, drastically reducing the amount of time the gang spent wandering the Fells. Maurice then took it a step further, using the birds of prey as spotters for animals who had ventured deep into the Fells, thereby creating opportunities for the gang to lie in wait and ambush their victims.

Cal remained hidden and watched a flicker of the hawk's shadow as it circled again and again, wondering if it was homing in on him, or if there was another unfortunate soul, injured or otherwise unaware they'd been spotted. He felt a sprinkle of debris against his head, looked away, and shielded his face as a cascade of dirt and pebbles rained down the cliff face. Brushing dirt from his shoulder, Cal looked up to see a weasel's snout poke over the edge of the cliff, sniffing, testing the air. The weasel wore a coarse brown sack like an oversized poncho, with a hood pulled tight over his head, nearly covering its eyes. Cal stayed in his low crouch and backed up, one paw on the wall, guiding him out as he focused on the weasel. He heard a snicker from behind and froze.

"Look what we got here," said a voice. Cal spun, ready for a fight. A massively muscled rat, sporting a cap over a tuft of hair and a large vest with too many pockets to count, blocked his path. The rat pushed himself up on his toes, puffed out his chest and grabbed a hold of a gnarled root from the base of the fallen tree. In one smooth motion he flexed and tore it free with a thick clod of dirt. He thumped the root, a make-shift club, against his paw, dirt raining free and showering him. He squinted, played tough as dirt hit him in the face and filled several of his vest pockets. "Boss told us the dog might come snooping around," he said, spitting a wad of dirt and phlegm. "He's always right, that boss."

"That's why he's boss," called the weasel from above. "Traitor dog."

Cal sighed in disbelief that these two knuckleheads had gotten the drop on him. He was off his game, his instincts dulled, even with his guard up. The pair was very young, conferring with each other through mumbled chittering that he couldn't quite catch. It sounded like they were debating whether or not to get support from the Rubbish Heap, or take him on themselves, eventually deciding on the latter. The weasel sent more debris raining down as he slid down the side, claws digging into the hill to slow his descent. When he landed on his feet, he drew a short knife from his belt and clutched it loosely at his hip.

Cal shifted to the side against the cliff face, swiveling his head, trying to keep an eye on both rodents, and said, "Then I'm sure you both know he visited me during the storm last night, and that we did not have a chance to finish our discussion."

"Look at 'im. Trying to lie his way past us already," Weasel said.

"Why would I lie? Come with me—you can ask him yourself," Cal said.

Weasel seemed to contemplate the idea for a moment, looked to Rat who continued his show of bravado, chewing on his tongue—a thin line of drool dripping down his chin.

"The boss visited you?" Weasel asked Cal—then to Rat, "Did you know about this?"

"Shut up, Weasel." Rat thumped his makeshift club against the ground. "We're done talking."

"Boss took you and not me, didn't he? Some 'midnight snack' you went out for." Weasel weakly scratched the cliff face with his knife, looking genuinely betrayed.

"Weasel."

"I trusted you."

"Weasel."

Cal raised his arms, palms up, calming the exchange between the two. He cleared his throat to prevent laughing at the absurdity of it all—the nostalgia of trying to manage incompetent fools. It was always the same with the rodents—he said, she said, fighting over this, that, and the other. It was exhausting trying to keep them in line and away from each other's throats; a bunch of grown children with sharp teeth, little memory, and even less foresight. It was a miracle that petty feuds didn't result in nightly attempts to burn down the Rubbish Heap. "I have no fight with you two. Leave me be and I'll be off to the Rubbish Heap. You can continue on your patrol and we'll pretend this never happened."

"We can't let you do that now, can we?" Rat said.

"Yeah, might get questioned about it. One of us is a terrible *liar*,"

Weasel said, glaring at his partner.

The rat raised his gnarled club and screeched, positioning himself to charge Cal. The weasel pointed his blade at the rat, at Cal, then back at the rat, chitter-chattering in short, angry bursts. The two went at it, back and forth, bickering over who got the first shot, Cal surmised. After a lengthy unintelligible discussion (during which Cal waited patiently, alert) the rat charged, raising his club high overhead as he sprinted at Cal's knees. Cal took a quick step forward to meet him. He kicked out, planting the ball of his foot against the rat's chest. The rat lost hold of the club, hat falling free from his head as the impact took the wind out of his lungs and sent him sprawling backwards into the mud.

The weasel looked to his downed friend and charged, swinging the short blade wildly from side to side in the tight space. Cal spun to face the attack, backing up as the weasel swung again and again. After several misses the weasel lunged at Cal, swinging in a wide arc. Cal ducked backwards, nearly tripping over the rat's club as the weasel's weapon flew within an inch of his nose. Weasel lost control of his swing, continued past Cal, and struck the underside of the tree, burying the blade to the hilt between a mass of tangled roots. Cal popped up and cracked the weasel across the jaw with a stiff punch as the rodent worked to free the blade. Cal shoved the stunned weasel against the cliff face, and ripped the blade from the tree, slipping past the weasel in the process. He grabbed a pawful of the weasel's shirt and pulled it to him, slipping the blade around Weasel's front and up against his throat, eliciting a yelp and a short piss that turned the dirt to mud between his quivering legs. Cal pulled the frightened weasel back from the mess, and growled as he locked eyes with the rat, still on his back, beginning to push himself up.

The rat collected his hat, dusting it off and giving it a detailed inspection before placing it back atop his head. He surveyed the mud coating his legs and back, appearing frustrated with the need to wipe it off, but resigned to his filthy fate. "You embarrass me, Weasel," he said, clapping the last of the dirt free from his claws. For a rat he had quite the obsession with cleanliness, a strange enough quirk to make Cal think they might have gotten along well years ago. The smell alone was often enough for him to give the squalid vermin a wide berth.

Cal shook with adrenaline, holding tight to the weasel as he processed the fight, the stress narrowing his vision as the memories instantly began to fade. He felt good, in control. But in many ways he'd gotten lucky, and it was a good thing they hadn't come at him together. His decision to confront Maurice on his own turf now gave him pause. He could handle two, but if another of the gang thought he could make a name for himself and the mob mentality turned on him, he didn't want to end up beaten and lost, deep in the Rubbish Heap—or worse. But he owed it to his dear Winifred, to his pups. He had to stay strong and move forward.

Cal barked at the rat to back up out of the trench, then ordered the weasel to march, pushing him out in front of him.

"What now, dog?" the rat asked, full of attitude, almost daring Cal to strike. "You got the drop on us."

"Yeah," mimicked the weasel, "What are you—"

Cal pressed the knife tighter against the weasel's throat, cutting him off. The weasel swallowed hard against the blade, leaking a few more drops of piss in the dead leaves at their feet. The rat's shoulders drooped in disappointment, eyes closed with a sigh. Cal played out the scenarios in his head, considered killing them both on the spot. The weasel would be easy—a quick flick of the wrist and he'd bleed out in seconds. The rat would run for it, but the macho rodent was as top heavy as they come, and Cal doubted he could scurry like the majority of his more svelte brothers and sisters. He didn't have time to bury them, other than to hide their bodies under a thin layer of dead leaves. The hawk still circled above, and even if it didn't tip off the Heap, another patrol would stumble on them eventually. Cal was still a good distance from his destination, and between that and the walk home, it was a lot to risk.

So are two idiots with hurt egos and big mouths, he thought. After a long moment lost in internal debate, Cal withdrew the blade from the weasel's neck, and kicked him in the behind, sending him stumbling forward to his knees beside the rat, who gracefully sidestepped to avoid helping his friend as he slid through the mud.

"You're going to continue your patrol," Cal ordered, blade reinforcing his tone. "You're not to speak of this. Not one word."

"Listen to him talk like he can just order us around," the weasel scoffed from his knees, arms and legs covered in muck.

The rat turned, slugged him in the gut, doubling him over. "But what about my blade?" the weasel whispered, clutching his stomach in pain.

"You lost it in the river," said the rat, "because you're an idiot."

"Enough!" Cal barked. "Go—both of you. Before I change my mind."

The rat dragged the weasel to his feet—careful to avoid his muddy limbs—and together they ran off. Cal watched them go, contemplating his decision. The pair barely made it a minute before the rat had to slow and catch his breath. The weasel looked back, eyes wide at Cal watching them, grabbed the rat by the vest, and dragged him on.

* * *

The light snow continued to flutter down from the sky, mostly melting as it reached the earth, the ground still too warm to hold it. Cal found a beauty in it, the way the wind gusts whirled the flurries between the trees, and wished he'd had Winifred there with him to share it with. He raised his head to let the tears roll back, collecting himself. Now wasn't the time.

When Cal was certain the rodents were gone, and the hawk with them, he abandoned the cover of the felled tree and continued his walk deeper into the Fells. He'd fallen into a trap of nostalgia and had let his guard down. He'd been so exhausted by the events of the recent days that the fire raging in his chest had shrunk to meager embers. But with each step he felt his focus returning, working himself up over the ambush, over Maurice invading his home, the vague threats against his family, the rumors, the truth about Winifred and the sickness that eluded him, and he felt the desire renew, the anger rise to the surface of his skin. It felt good. He wanted to hurt Maurice, to break him and make him suffer for setting foot in the Woods.

Despite Cal's eagerness for action, the remainder of the trek to the Rubbish Heap was uneventful. Deep down he was thankful. There was only one of him and the Rubbish Heap could hold a legion of all manner of rodents. Cal caught a whiff well before it came into view—a biting stench that stung his nose and made his eyes water. Somehow it was worse than memory served. It rose in the distance, a monstrous lumpy hill established in a clearing that had been widened in Cal's absence. It had taken on the look of an enormous beaver dam, if said dam was clustered in a pile and covered with all manner of detritus so matted that even during dry spel s it appeared damp.

As Cal crept closer to the mound, a loud commotion erupted near the front, many voices fighting over each other to be heard. Instead of continuing to the front, he cut to his right, taking a long way to approach from the side. When he caught sight of the argument, he dropped, prone, crawling through a cluster of young pine.

The pine "trees," if one could even call them such, appeared more like bushes in their infancy—hundreds sprouting out of the decay to form a hazy green cloud. Cal tried to avoid them as he pulled himself along with his forearms, but there were so many that it was impossible for him not to bend a few beneath him as he passed, hoping that the movement didn't alert guards as he approached the edge of the cluster.

From his hiding place within the pine he could see the entrance, and his heart sunk. There were nearly two dozen of the gang—weasels, opossums, rats, even a squirrel—of all shapes, colors, and sizes bickering with each other. It appeared a patrol had returned empty handed, and the next to go out was giving them hell for it. The rat and weasel he'd confronted earlier were nowhere to be found, actually heeding his warning to them and staying away, but there were too many to make a move. Even if he singled out one of the leaders and attempted to talk his way in, there were too many to risk the possibility of things going south—and this time there would be more coming at him. Cal lay still, contemplating his options when his ears perked up, picking up a soft hum that echoed in his memory.

The cold wind blows hmm hmm hmm
Tie a knot around a finger
So it goes hmm hmm
Don't you linger
Hmm hmm . . . the night is comin'
Bellies are a rumblin' hmm hmm
Only an old crone hmm hmm
Brings a spoon and a stone hmm hmm

Cal shifted among the pines, slowly crawling across them to

the far side where the soft voice originated. Peeling back the last of the trees blocking his view, he couldn't help but smile when he saw the performer.

A thin pygmy shrew in a plain dark-blue dress tapped a pine needle cane against the ground as she whispered her tune. Bending down, she reached into the leaves to snatch a large black ant. It wiggled in her paw, flailing its limbs. The shrew gave it a good shake and popped it head-first into her mouth. As Cal watched, she suddenly stopped mid-chew, spitting out the pulped insect. She craned her neck up and stuck her nose out, sniffing the air. Her old eyes drew wide and she dropped her needle cane in shock.

"Oh, my lynn," she said, still looking up. "If it ain't my favorite mutt. I used to be able to smell you coming from a mile away." She gave her nose a supportive pat. "I must be getting old."

"Regina," Cal said. "You don't look a day older than when I left."

Regina had already lived in the Rubbish Heap for years when Cal stumbled upon the grounds. The tough shrew took him under her wing, ensuring he was not taken advantage of too much, though she herself was a constant source of grief, bumping into walls, making a mess in the Heap's makeshift kitchen and filling his head with stories that he could never tell were true or not. Like how she came to be at the Heap. She was young, she'd said, blind from birth with only her loving family to keep her alive when most would have left her to die. Her family had been out gathering food for the coming winter when they stumbled into the Fells and were captured by Maurice and a posse of vermin. Supposedly her father tried to cut a deal with Maurice, offering up Regina as stew meat if they let the rest of them go. Maurice felt sorry for Regina and angry with her father for offering to sacrifice his daughter. He lost it, devouring him on the spot and boiling her brothers and sisters upon their return.

Maurice offered to return Regina to her home, but she stuck around, for what is a blind shrew to do? She'd left Cal in shock, but she'd also laughed long and hard after, so Cal never knew the real story. Maurice wouldn't comment on it either, saying he'd heard her make up so many variations that he no longer recalled the truth.

While helping her prepare meals, Cal grew to love her dark sense of humor. She was one of the very few things he missed from his former life.

The shrew smiled at the mention of her name. "Oh, stop it. Would you believe me if I told you I hadn't heard that name in years? The rubbish call me Old Auntie Shrew and trample my precious dandelions."

"That's no way to treat the wisest cook in the Fells."

"You're telling me. When they get me all riled up I serve bugs, and tonight the menu is all six-legged." She gestured to a large wicker basket she'd stuffed with all manner of insect—ants, crickets, beetles, and pillbugs—each missing its head, to which she commented, "I don't let them have the best parts, of course."

"That'll serve them right."

"For a couple days. Then too many thoughts will clog their brains and they'll go back to forgetting how to hold account of themselves." Regina coughed and cleared her throat. "These ants are dry, too. Going to need some water to wash them down. Good thing there is plenty to go around. What brings you out to the river? I was just going to have a nice sit alongside it but I have yet to find it."

Cal lay stunned for a moment, unsure how to respond given they were nowhere near the river. When he opened his mouth to speak, she cut him off, said, "I'm just messing with you. I may be blind but I know this place. The more things change around here, the more they stay the same."

There was more truth in that than Cal wanted to believe.

Regina stabbed her cane back into the leaves, narrowly missing another ant that scuttled quickly away. She cursed the insect, hissing between a narrow gap in her teeth.

"How's the family? What happened to bring you out all this way?"

"Oh, they're good," Cal said, suddenly wishing to end the conversation, the appeal of their encounter having run its course.

"Good, huh?" She took another stab at an ant, plunging her cane through the sweet spot between its head and thorax. She twisted the cane with both hands, popping the head off. "Don't lie to me, Cal. My ears make up for my eyes, you know—often more than I care for."

"I'm looking for Maurice."

"Of course, only you won't find him here. He's gone south for the day. Sounds like he's making the rounds."

"Why? He was never one to enjoy leaving the Fells for long. At one point I thought he might have been afraid to stray far from the Rubbish Heap. You're telling me he's gone as far as the bog?"

"I can't say. Didn't hear much except for him putting the guards on notice that he'd be out for a bit. Doesn't like to give them much detail, you know. Keeps them guessing enough to postpone any dreams of grandeur."

Cal looked up at the sky, pinpointing the faded sun through the clouds. The bog was a hike from the Fells, but if he hurried he could make it. The boys would be late again, working with Billiam to finish prepping for the Moon Festival. That gave him the afternoon and most of the early evening before he needed to be home and ready to receive them. The thought of being confronted again about their mother filled him with dread. He could only string the lies along for so long until hope was completely replaced with distrust, a deadline part of him worried had already passed.

"Watch your back, Cal. He's up to something."

The old friends exchanged parting pleasantries, Cal holding out a paw and Regina giving it a hug and a poke with her needle cane for good measure, followed by a hearty laugh. Cal crawled back through the pines, listening to Regina return to humming her songs. When he got to the edge he stood and ran.

8

The cold westerly wind rolled across the meadow, churning its tall grasses like waves in the sea, ushering them toward a distant shore. Gus took shelter at the meadow's edge, leaning against a naked elm tree. The temperature had fallen since they left the school, his breathing emitted white wisps. He watched a pair of larks flit across the clearing, dipping in and out of the grasses, squalls tossing them carelessly about like wooden toys. Franklin lay on the ground beside him, head propped on his backpack, looking up at the sky. The brothers had run from the school without stopping or looking back. Gus's complaints about forgetting to grab his boots, to slow down, or to pause and catch their breath had been ignored until they reached the clearing, where inexplicably, Franklin stopped and took a seat. Perhaps it was the sight of the forbidden Fells, or memories of time spent in the meadow with their father. Gus wasn't sure. He could tell his older brother didn't feel like talking, so he left it alone. When the birds disappeared, Gus placed his pack on the ground, mimicking his brother's setup, and laid down beside him.

"It's warmer down here," Gus said, having settled in.

"Why do you think I'm lying down, dummy?" Franklin replied. "I'm not that tired."

The pair lay in silence for a while, until Gus again piped up. "What are you looking at?"

"I think it's going to snow." Franklin pointed a finger at the sky, tracing the edge of a gray front. "Those are snow clouds."

"It's too early for snow."

"Frances told me it once snowed in August. Anything is possible, if it gets cold enough."

"Frances is a liar." Gus hugged his arms across his chest; the initial respite from the wind was fleeting.

"Not everything a fox says is a lie. You've been letting Beatrix get inside your head."

"Have not! It's not my fault I sit near her, and that Nutbrown makes us work together all the time."

"Have too—and if she messes with you again I'm going let her have it, right in those big buck teeth."

"But—"

"I don't care what Nutbrown does. If she can whip our hides, she can whip that beaver's tail too." Franklin turned his head to face Gus as he spoke, his eyes damp, voice subtly cracking. "No one talks to you that way, especially about our mother."

Gus looked to his brother, even after he'd turned back to face the sky, blinking back tears. The brothers were quiet again for a time, the soft sound of the wind filling the space between them until Gus reached over, taking Franklin's paw in his own.

"Mom's not going to be okay, is she?" Gus asked, his voice a choked whisper, filled with defeat.

Franklin sniffled, and after a time, said, "I don't know."

"Do you think she's out there? Alone?" These thoughts had been on Gus's mind since he'd gone back to bed in the early morning hours, but to hear them aloud stunned him, as if his fears were suddenly made real.

"I don't know."

"What do you mean, you don't know?" Gus pushed himself up to his knees, more upset with himself than Franklin. After all, he was the one who provided the image of their mother suffering alone and thus somehow responsible for her fate—unless Franklin would refute it. "You always know!"

Franklin ignored his outburst, rubbed his eyes dry with balled paws. He rolled over, grabbing his pack as he stood.

"Let's get going. We're wasting time." Franklin started into the meadow, holding up an arm to shield his face.

Gus scrambled to catch up with him, shouting into the wind. "Where are we going?"

"To see Old Brown," Franklin yelled back over his shoulder.

"What? *Old Brown?* Why? Dad would kill us if he found out! We're not supposed to cross the river."

"Because Mom works for him."

Gus sprinted after his brother, grabbed him by the pack and swung him around to confront him face-to-face. "What are you talking about?"

"I saw them together once, Mom and Old Brown. When I was little—you were still a baby. I snuck off while Dad was feeding you."

"And?"

"I got scared. Old Brown was furious when he saw me. I wouldn't stop crying after he left, so Mom sat me down and explained that he was good and she was just doing him some favors."

"Favors?"

Franklin shrugged. "I didn't ask. She said it was for Dad and that no one else could know, including him. It was our secret, so I kept it to myself."

Gus tried to read his brother's face, unable to focus as thoughts swirled in his head. Franklin had shared something special with their mother, and although the event was strange and a bit scary, Gus felt left out—like being picked last for an activity at school, stuck to dawdle alone until a team was forced to draft him.

"Your secret," Gus whispered. He held nothing of the sort, not even a hole dug behind the house to hide some childish trinket.

"Hey." Franklin put a paw on his brother's shoulder. "This will be our secret, okay? Just you and me. No one else will know about this trip. We'll tell Dad we went for a long walk to cool off."

Gus nodded, barely able to look his brother in the eye. Yes, they were about to cross into the Fells, something their father had strictly forbidden, but the "secret" felt phony, manufactured. Of course they wouldn't tell anyone—neither of them wanted to get in trouble. They had enough coming when they returned to school.

A sprinkle of flurries whisked down out of the sky, landing on Gus's jacket before quickly melting.

"See? Told you it was going to snow," Franklin said, grinning at the white flakes.

"You could have told me!"

"I did!" Franklin turned and continued across the field toward the fallen log.

Gus chased after him, shaking his head. They both knew he wasn't talking about the snow.

* * *

Despite Gus's reservations, the two crossed the log with ease, sliding across its slick trunk to the other side and setting foot in the Fells without an adult for the first time (that Gus could remember). Franklin said there had been other times, of course, but Gus had no recollection of the trips. As they ventured northwest toward the base of Old Brown's mount, everything felt new, yet older than anything he'd witnessed in his short life. The trees seemed to grow taller there, but compared to the Woods it lacked something—warmth; a soul.

"Everything is . . . dead," Gus heard himself whisper.

"Winter is coming, dummy," said Franklin. "What do you expect?"

There was more to it than dead leaves and gray clouds. The packed layers of decay beneath their feet. The way the trees grew straight in comparison to their sickly branches that began toward the top of the trunks like a foreign species: curving, bending, fighting for sunlight. The frail pines wilting against one another; untouched, explosive growth giving way to clusters of tiny shrub-like things that fought each other for nutrients. It was all wild and unkempt, and it scared Gus. It's not as if the Woods were a manicured paradise, but the residents took care of their backyard. Here things were different—abandoned.

They made their way over small hills, past huge chunks of rock set at odd angles as if they'd exploded from the earth. While neither of them spoke, the quiet didn't strike Gus as odd until he heard a sharp cry that froze him in his tracks. Startled, he looked up to see a hawk coasting above them, circling, its wings outstretched wide.

"I don't like this, Franklin. We should head back."

"It's just a bird. They fly over the Woods too, you know. Doubt they have parents restricting where they can fly."

His brother waved him on, continuing ahead a few steps around a bend, only to suddenly vanish with a yelp.

Gus ran forward, shouting for his brother. "Franklin! Where'd you go?"

"Down here!" came a reply.

Gus skidded to a stop at the edge of a well-concealed hole. Even to the untrained eye it was clear the hole was a trap—hand-dug and nearly twice the depth of Franklin's height. And wide too. It had been engineered to catch something big.

"Are you okay?"

Franklin dusted himself off. His foot was sore, but he'd caught the edge of the hole with a paw on the way down and had slowed his descent enough to soften the landing. They were lucky there was nothing at the bottom but the leaves and branches used to camouflage the pit. When they were younger, older kids had scared them with stories of their friends disappearing into pits laden with all manner of spikes, drowning mud, and other assurances of death.

Gus crouched down at the edge, and leaned in, extending his paw as far as he could. "Grab on."

Franklin jumped and caught hold of Gus's paw. "Pull me up!"

"I'm trying!" Gus clenched his teeth, flattening out as he strained every ounce of muscle in his body, demanding it pull his brother to safety. But Franklin's weight was too much and he began to pull Gus down with him. Gus flailed about and dug in his toes, his free paw finding nothing but dirt and leaves for support.

"Let go let go let go!" Gus yelled. Franklin released his grip and Gus caught himself on the edge, seconds before he would have fallen in.

"Try and find a branch," Franklin offered.

"Good idea." Gus pushed himself up to his knees to find two strangers walking toward him, watching him from the other side of the hole. He felt an instinctive growl in his throat as his nose caught a whiff of the approaching vermin. Their father had warned them since they were born: there were no good vermin. The rat and weasel staring him down fit the warning.

"What are you waiting for? Go!" Franklin said, before Gus shushed him.

"Well look what we got here, Rat. The apple doesn't fall far from the tree. Get it?" The vermin gave Gus a once-over before walking to the edge of the hole and looking over to see Franklin at the bottom.

"*Apples*. There are two of 'em."

"I was making a joke—"

"Shut up, idiot. You're lucky we stayed out as long as we did. If we had stuck to the path—"

"We wouldn't have run into these two."

"His kids."

"Whose kids?"

The rat slapped a paw over his face, shaking his head. "Who do you think? Weren't you proud of your dumb apple joke?"

"Yeah! We found one dog and here are two mo—"

One dog? The words flashed through Gus's head, igniting hope. Could they have seen their mother? Was she close?

Gus could actually see the light bulb go on in the weasel's brain, and it scared him. The rodent's face darkened and he scrambled around the pit toward Gus, snatching him by his coat before Gus could do more than put his paws up in surrender. The weasel pulled him in close, giving him a good look at Weasel's teeth and a dose of spoiled breath before leaning him over the side of the hole.

"How about that?" Weasel said. "I knew something good was due to come our way. What do you say we clean 'em up right here?"

"I'd say that's a great idea, Weasel, seeing as how too much talk has left us once again humiliated."

"Speak for yourself. I'd say we're more than redeemed. I'm going to enjoy this on a personal level."

Gus flailed in the weasel's arms, feet on the edge of the hole. Franklin screamed for help, to leave Gus alone and let them go.

"We're looking for our mother!" Gus blurted. "Have you seen her?"

"Gus!" Franklin tried to wave his brother off, but their secret was already out.

"A mother, eh?" Weasel lowered Gus to the edge, keeping a tight grip on his jacket with one paw. "Mister Rat, I think this one means to tell us we might bag the entire family."

"Kids are enough for me. These feet have seen enough today."

"Better get started then." Weasel pulled a stick from his belt, the end sharpened to a deadly point. He tossed it up, flipping it end over end. Gus cringed, closed his eyes as it came down, waiting for the inevitable. He heard a *thunk*, and a gasp. Something warm and wet sprayed against his face, a bitter scent blooming in his nose. He opened his eyes to see a good two inches of a harpoon's crimson-stained tip emerge from the weasel's chest, nearly brushing up against his jacket.

Shock flooded through Gus, strapping his legs in place. The weasel looked down at the bolt in disbelief, gave the tip a tap with his stick, and coughed blood across the pup's feet. Gus started at the grotesque sight, finding himself in time to step to the side just as the weasel pitched forward, head-first into the hole. Franklin yelped, flattening himself against the wall as the body landed with a thud, crumpled and motionless beside him.

"Duck." Gus dropped to the ground at the sound of a familiar voice. He looked away from the sound, over the hole, to see the rat turn and run for his life. The rat didn't make it more than a few steps before another harpoon caught him in the thigh, punching him forward and pinning him to the ground. He screamed, slamming his oversized arms into the hard earth, desperately trying to free himself. The harpoon was deep and the earth unforgiving. Gus watched as George Washington, a most regal toad, stepped forward from behind a tree, wordlessly stalking toward the downed rat. In trained, fluid motions, GW loaded another harpoon from a quiver over his shoulder as he moved, never taking his eyes off his victim. The rat pushed and pushed and finally as the harpoon began to slide from the ground, GW reached him, stepping on top of it like a stepstone, forcing it back down as he moved onto the rat's back. The rat screamed in agony. GW put his other foot on the rat's lower back, readied the gun and fired, the harpoon punching through the rat between his shoulder blades. The rat twitched one last gasp and lay still. The toad loaded his last harpoon, clutching the weapon tightly between his webbed fingers as he scanned the surroundings.

Appearing satisfied with the situation, GW asked if there were any more. When neither pup spoke up, he looked to Gus, who shook his head, and then down into the hole at Franklin.

"You okay?" he asked, lowering the butt of the gun to Franklin.

Franklin nodded. "Think you could give the bolt in the weasel's back a tug and see if it will slide free? Ah, nevermind. Grab a hold and I'll get you out." GW groaned as he pulled him out, the strain visible on his face. Once Franklin was out, GW turned to Gus, said, "What about you? You good?"

Gus nodded, muttering a difficult, "Yes, sir."

"You both know the rules. Regardless of what you think you might be going through, you *never, ever* set foot in the Fells. Is that clear?"

They both nodded.

"I didn't hear you."

A duo of yes-sirs and never-again-sirs stumbled from their quivering mouths.

"We're going to march right back to school and you're going to apologize to Missus Nutbrown. Now get to. I'll be right behind you."

Gus slung his bag over his shoulder, hugged Franklin by the arm and moved, spurred on by the terrible sound of GW wrenching the harpoons free from the rat.

GW held up one of the projectiles, inspecting the bloodied tip, said to himself, "Now, *where* is your father?"

9

Clem lay sprawled against the far wall of the cell, the room shrouded in near total darkness—the only source of light a dusty jar of glowing insects she'd discovered abandoned after her meal. She waved her free arm back and forth, playing with the chain attached to the shackle on her wrist, dragging it across the bare floor. She wasn't sure why, but she enjoyed the clink of the chain links, the rough oompf sound they made when she whipped them against the dirt—though since she'd first awoke in the room, she wasn't sure of many things, like why the raccoon fell a with the eye-patch insisted on calling her Clem, and the notion that she was somehow his cousin, which seemed downright impossible. She didn't much care for the name, but since the madness had taken hold—her term for it—the fever spells becoming more and more frequent, leaving her with terrifying blackouts, she'd been unable to recall her previous name, or if she'd indeed had one at all. The raccoon was nice enough, but he hadn't explained why she was chained (had he?) and left alone, forbidden visitors. Still, she eagerly awaited his return. The thought of spending the remainder of her days alone was too much to bear.

The "meal" the raccoon had brought her lay shattered in a corner of the room, pieces of the skull piled like a small cairn, a game she'd played in the darkness out of boredom. She'd picked the head clean, cracked the skull and tasted the brain, eventually eating it in its entirety, licking the inside of the cavity. As she remembered little, she must have been delirious from one of her spells, and any attempt at recollection roiled her stomach, pushing the taste of bile to the back of her tongue. As sick as she was (and she was sick, enough to fill her with dreadful anticipation of what might become of her if and when the symptoms worsened) she swore she'd never eat raw rabbit again. When the raccoon returned—oh, how she prayed he would, and soon—she'd have a talk with him. Some tea with milk would be her first order of business, something to calm her nerves. Then maybe something simple—some nice, crusty bread to ease her stomach, followed by something to take the edge off.

Clem stretched her right arm out, pulling the chain taut from the wall. Midway through her meal she'd attempted to rip it free, but it refused to budge. The other chain had come free so easily that her failure to free her right arm nearly drove her mad, biting at her wrist below the shackle until it bled and the pain shocked her senses. Her old bones ached with the torment of frigid winters. She desperately wished to free herself, but she was tired, so tired, and the more stress she put on the chain, the more sleep called to her. A nap couldn't hurt, she told herself. She'd feel better if she closed her eyes for a few. She prodded the glass jar, the lightning bugs flitting about in response, emitting their warm glow.

Who knows? Maybe someone would be there to greet her when she woke . . .

* * *

Fog-filled dreams came to Clem in fits and spurts. The creaking of old wagon wheels on dirt roads. The smell of spring grass. The clip-clop of hooves. Bits of song, a female voice so familiar, yet unknown and without a name.

> *O'er the hills and through the Woods*
> *We sell our wares and take our goods*
> *Our trusty steed does lead us on*
> *Best friends we'll make until we're gone*

The voice—she whistled against the wind. The creaking of old wagon wheels. The smell of dead leaves. Wood smoke. A stinging, biting pain. Swelling, throbbing in her skull. A tingling heat that traveled down her spine, out toward her limbs. She gasped.

* * *

Clem startled awake clutching her throat, drenched in sweat, sweet memories from her dreams vanishing in a flash. Her tongue felt big for her mouth, rough and too dry to swallow without her throat screaming in protest. She tried to push herself up, to stand and leave the room, but her legs shook uncontrollably, and she had forgotten she was shackled to the wall. The pressure inside her head seemed to grow with each throb of her heart. She screamed, pounding her fists against the floor. Everything hurt. She wanted, *needed* to die. Suddenly vivid in her mind, the sensation of the chain popping loose from the wall. She *needed* to be free; needed to find someone—the raccoon. She was dying; she could feel it. *Not here. Not alone.* And with that, all rational thought vanished.

She grabbed hold of the remaining chain, pulled with all her strength, again bracing her feet against the crude floor. She felt the temperature in her brain rising as she pulled, her blood boiling. She screamed again and again, her voice monstrously hoarse. Letting go of the chain, she focused on the shackle around her wrist, the intense pain as she ripped, and ripped and ripped again, trying to force her paw through too small a hole. But she continued, again and again, the shackle, slick with blood and sweat, slipping up onto her paw, bending it into an unnatural 'U' shape as she tried to force the numb appendage through. She put her feet up against the wall, wailing as she pulled with her core, legs, stomach, back—then suddenly, she felt herself flying backwards, landing with a thud to the sound of glass shattering beside her.

Taking deep breaths, she held up her damaged paw, half-expecting it to be gone, a stump draining the last bit of her life. But it was there, bloodied and numb. It hurt to move, even a whisper, sending jolts of pain down her wrist. As she gritted her teeth, testing her fingers, the fireflies, free from captivity, fluttered to the ceiling, bouncing about until finding their way to the exit. Clem scrambled to her feet, ignoring the pain, to follow them into the dark corridor. Up ahead came shouts of alarm as figures rushed into view. The leader, a skinny thing with a long neck, stopped short of Clem, holding the others back. The look of fear in their eyes at the sight of her was something to behold. She licked her lips, tasted blood.

Hungry, she thought. *Hungry*.

10

While the Woods proper ran like a well-oiled ecological machine in accordance with the sun and seasons, the farther south one traveled, to the bog and below, the more time became less of a dictator, and more of belligerent guardian attempting (and often failing) to enforce its rules upon society. The annual cycle of death and rebirth went swimmingly, for the most part, though all stages seemed to occur at the same time throughout, giving way to a constant air of pungent sweetness, humidity, and decay. Karl's Drinkery, the sole watering hole to serve the bog denizens (and those from the Woods and beyond who made the trek) was a prime example. No one quite knew who (or what) Karl was, and aside from the name being carved into all sorts of nooks and crannies within, there was no written record of the name. To add to the confusion, the regular barkeep, Karly, an attractive muskrat (by muskrat standards), ran the place, though the patrons were almost exclusively amphibian and reptile bog dwellers. A few regulars known to partake in a thimble of grog too many often enjoyed attempts at ordering a nightcap from "Karl" and would receive a snap of a bar towel to the throat from the lady muskrat for the offense.

There'd been attempts to change the name to avoid this confusion, but the old guard always shouted it down (*But tradition!* Or, *She's a mammal for bogs-sake!* Or, *Think of the children!* —which always elicits the most laughs). Today, most referred to it as the Drinkery as a sign of respect.

Built into an ancient grotto, the inside was surprisingly large, featuring a long bar and a handful of tables. Dozens of candles were spread throughout along the walls, behind the bar and across the tables providing a dim light that made for a cozy atmosphere. While the space was roomy, the entrance was quite small in comparison—a rounded door that prevented the larger species of mammals from entering (which the regulars did not view as not a bad thing by any means).

Karly ran a paw over her forehead, combing fur back over her left ear and out of her eyes. It was early in the evening, but the day had been exceptionally busy, keeping her attentive and on her toes, sending for her lizard barback to pull a double shift. She blamed it on the weather, as each patron had commented on the unexpected cold when they'd come in the door. The annual transition from late fall into winter packed the Drinkery, as it was always warm with a pleasant touch of humidity (thanks to the subterranean cave system beneath the grotto) and there was little to do for the bog folk who stuck around, other than survive and dream of the spring thaw.

She poured two fresh thimbles of grog, pushing them across the bar to Robinson. The lizard flicked his tongue out in acknowledgment of his boss before carefully delivering the drinks to a couple of romantic frogs nestled in one of the back corners.

"I hear you," Karly muttered to herself. She made another mental note to give Robinson an extra share of the night's tips when they closed up. She watched the young frogs clink drinks, and toast each other. It was their third date at the pub (yes, she'd counted) and she felt a twinge of jealousy at the flash of love in their eyes. She pulled a rag from her waist and gave the bar a gentle rub down. It's you and me, pal, she thought, smiling. Her work was something to be proud of.

* * *

The door opened, the tinny ring of the small bell above the entrance announcing the latest guests. First Mildred, a black salamander with splotches of yellow down her back, sporting a velvet collared jacket. Hank strode in behind her, the tortoise turning sideways to slip his shell cleanly through the opening.

". . . and the squirrel had to give the kids an early morning recess because she was so beside herself," he said as he removed his cap, hanging it on one of several hooks beside the door. "Can you believe that? Kids pick up on this sort of thing, you know. I wouldn't be surprised if more of them act up with the intent of cutting class short."

"Oh, hush. Give the woman a break. I only have myself to worry about, and I'm half exhausted by nightfall." Mildred gave a slight wave to Robinson, held up two digits to Karly, who nodded and went to work. "You try and deal with a roomful of misfits day in, day out."

"No, thank you. Clayton is more than enough. Myrtle wants more, but I keep telling her—why fix what isn't broke?"

The old friends grabbed seats at their regular table near the center of the Drinkery, facing the bar and the entrance.

"And how's that working out for you?" Mildred asked, pushing herself in.

Hank laughed, his head and neck bobbing in his shell. "About as well as you'd imagine. I'm liable to be crawling with little ones come spring."

Robinson arrived with their grog, giving Mildred a quick wink and hello as he set her cup down. She smiled, thanking him for the drink. Hank raised an eyebrow, giving her a look as he raised his cup.

"Don't you even," she started, "it's nothing." If salamanders could blush she would've been flaring red. She and Robinson had had a fling when they were younger, though they'd cooled off nearly as fast as they'd heated up. The breakup left Mildred embarrassed and less apt to discuss her relationships, even with close friends. But recently the pair had rekindled some of their heat, getting together twice in the last week for a midnight snack under the moon. It felt good—more than good, in fact—but she wasn't going to jinx it by bringing it up, especially with Hank, who would find too much enjoyment in teasing her until it inevitably (in her mind) fell apart all over again.

Hank grinned at his small victory, toasted, "To babies."

"*Your* babies," Mildred said, quick to correct. "Enjoy it while we got it."

* * *

GW marched south through the Woods, shoulders back, chin up, chest out—full of renewed vigor. He pumped his arms as he walked, harpoons jangling against each other on his back, humming a mix of old battle hymns. He hadn't felt so alive since he'd been in the thick of it during the war, weaving in and out of mangroves, holding fast beside his brothers and sisters. He shuddered thinking of the invasive species of snake that nearly wiped out the southern reaches, the monstrous *Python bivittatus*. GW shuddered, a cold sweat dampening his limbs as nightmarish flashbacks threatened to steal his high, but his adrenaline rush was too great, too positive to be beaten. Now look at him, he thought, Sir George Washington, a most regal toad—a most regal *hero*. The sound of it was music to his ears.

The fight in the Fells was a mere blip in his memory. He replayed the action in his head as he marched, filling in the gaps as the shock wore off and the details returned. He'd left the rodent's bodies where they lay, prioritizing the safety and rescue of the pups. Hidden or out in the open, they'd be discovered and scavenged by nightfall. The dead were never lonely for long. In the aftermath, the youngest pup, Gus (as GW had to be reminded of twice, having always had difficulty with names while under stress), pointed out the hawk circling above them, and it pained

GW to have missed scouting the bird. He'd grown rusty, perhaps even complacent in his role as guardian of the school—unforgivable in life-or-death situations. But he had risen to the occasion and was quite pleased with the results aside from the aerial miss. He'd heard enough about the Rubbish Heap vermin to know the hawk was likely a trained spotter, and would report their activity and location to its leadership. However, he quickly determined it to be well out of range, and again, his priority was the safety of the pups and their return to the school. Tracking and pursuit of the bird was for another day, another mission. (And if he were honest with himself, deep down he'd be perfectly fine to never set foot in the Fells again.)

The trek back to the Woods was uneventful and quiet aside from the boys' occasional small talk between them. GW caught bits and pieces of their story, or at least the story they were concocting, regarding their reasons for crossing the river. He did his best to remain uninterested. Discipline wasn't his job (he'd already given them enough shame in the moment to contemplate during the walk) and between Nutbrown and their parents, there was more than enough awaiting them back home. Instead, GW stayed focused on the environment, making use of the event to practice maintaining a heightened awareness—head on a swivel, harpoon gun at the ready.

It was late in the afternoon when they neared the school. The pups were exhausted, packs weighing heavily upon their shoulders. The older pup pleaded with GW to let them go finish their decorations for the Moon Festival. "The badger will be there," he'd said, "and he'll help get us home." But GW owed it to their parents, to the community, to return them safely to the school, where they'd been last seen. He saw through their thin facade of bravery. They needed discipline and comfort if they were to pull through the day's events.

At the edge of the school clearing, Nutbrown saw them coming and emerged from the one-room building, arms tight across her chest, face a mask of restrained anger. The pups recoiled at the sight of her, but GW ushered them on, and offered to stay and say his part if need be. But when they reached the school, their teacher ordered them inside to sit alone while the adults discussed their actions. GW relayed the events to the best of his recollection. The squirrel showed little interest or respect for his story, at one point interrupting him over concerns that he'd left his post, jeopardizing the safety of the entire class for the fate of two troublemakers. GW was so flabbergasted at her quip that he was left speechless.

"Is that all?" she'd asked as she departed, refusing GW's offer to be present with the pups during her reprimand, in their father's absence. She'd cut him off before he could explain the benefits of his involvement. "Your place is out here, *guard*," she'd said, stabbing a finger at his barrel. He'd glared at her during the short outburst. Any past enjoyment of her classroom tirades was colored now that he was the target. *How dare she!* he'd thought. He remained silent, taking it as he had from barking drill sergeants—back straight, emotionless, staring at the spot between her eyes. If anything, she might wear herself out on him and leave little for the pups.

"*Is that all?* " He repeated her remark, scoffing at the old squirrel's audacity. If it weren't for the kids and his fierce loyalty to duty, he would have spun on his heels and never returned. He needed a celebratory drink, an early night, and sweet dreams to maintain the rush and prevent her from dragging him down. Tomorrow morning he'd be back at his post, ready to greet the children and welcome them—with a smile—to a new day. If the squirrel was going to double-down on being a sourpuss, he'd stick it to her, all right. Not all wars were fought and won with weapons.

GW grinned eardrum to eardrum as he marched onward, quite pleased with himself, belting out in song that startled a pair of finches resting nearby and scattered them into the trees.

> "*A drink, but a drink, but a drink's all I need.*
> *Go and offer me your best, but I'll settle for the mead.*
> *Spare me the protest, for honey helps digest . . .*"

Hank and Mildred clinked thimbles as the tinny bell rang again, signaling a newcomer. The door to the Drinkery swung wide, hinges creaking as it came to a stop. After a short pause, drawing the attention of the patrons to the empty doorway, GW leapt inside. He stuck the landing, slapping his feet against the damp floor, standing tall, webbed hands at his hips. "Good evening, fellow boggies! Next round is on me." He gave Karly a thumbs up, closed the door, and turned to the wall hooks, unzipping his outermost layer in one swoop.

"Wait a minute . . ." Hank glanced around the pub for a nonexistent clock. "Either you're early, or . . ." Hank tipped his thimble to his mouth, draining the grog in two gulps. His face contorted as the fiery liquid washed down his throat, but he kept a niggling coughing fit to a minimum. "We seem to have lost ourselves in conversation and fallen behind. Bartender! I'll partake in this gentle-toad's generous offer. One for himself as well, please." The tortoise looked to Mildred, who shook her head.

"Don't give me that look," she said. "You know I'm a sipper." The salamander took the smallest of sips, as if to emphasize the point.

"Relax, shed your coat. GW's hanging up his third layer."

"Second," GW said over his shoulder. "Scarves aren't layers."

Hank pressed a hand to his chest. "Apologies, my warmly dressed friend. Consider me informed."

"Spare me." GW finished removing his second layer, a thin windbreaker, which he threw over his shoulder to reorganize his belongings over one hook. First the scarf, then the windbreaker, and last, the down winter coat. Finally, he slipped out of his snow pants, which he hung beside the coats, leaving him wearing gray long underwear and a red vest, with gold trim and a regal collar, zipped to his chin. "Trade you for your shell," he said, taking a seat across from his old friends.

"You know I would," Hank said, giving the shell a tug around his wrinkly neck, "but I'm a bit attached. Besides, the kids would play tricks on you, knock you on your back, leave you stuck and all that. I'll save you the embarrassment. Do you know how long it took me to learn how to roll myself back onto my stomach?"

"Humor me."

"Too long. Look at this face." Hank highlighted a superficial scar on the side of his face. "The emotional scars run deep. I get a little off balance and the flashbacks hit me like a ton of rocks."

"Your parents taught you how to roll over, you goof." Mildred snickered. "You ran to school the next day to show us your new 'survival' skills before class."

"Is that so? Must have blocked out the torture."

"I distinctly recall your father boasting you'd mastered the skill in one night."

"Well, he had a penchant for embellishing a story."

"No," GW said, feigning surprise.

"It's true."

Mildred rolled her eyes. "Like father, like son. Anyway . . ." she said, moving on to GW, "How was your day? Catch any interesting gossip?"

"Good, actually," GW said, unable to hide a smile. "It was very good."

"I'll say—with that entrance it must have been something."

Robinson delivered their drinks, passing out fresh thimbles of grog and collecting Hank's empty.

"Must have been busy—didn't see you when I picked up the lad. Squirrel send you off to collect some nuts? Mammals finally learn to protect themselves?" Hank laughed hard at his own joke, cheering GW and Mildred's thimbles with his own.

Karly dropped a thimble she was drying on the bar, the clang grabbing the patrons' attention. Hank turned to find her glaring at him. The Drinkery was no place for mammal jokes. Not while she was working, at least.

"Okay, then." Hank turned his attention back to the table, clearing his throat. "Where were we?"

"I believe you were rudely taking away GW's chance to talk about his wonderful day," Mildred said. "I heard it was snowing. Did you see snow?" She shivered on her seat. "I'm not ready for the cold."

"Flurries." GW's thoughts drifted back to the Fells, crouched on the side of the path. The way the dim sunlight caught on the snowflakes, floating down as he tucked the harpoon gun against his shoulder and took aim at the weasel, patiently lining up his shot. "There were some flurries to the north, but nothing stuck."

"That's good to hear."

"It is, but what of it?" Hank took another gulp, slamming down his cup. "It snows every year. I want to know about today. Spill, my most regal friend!"

GW glanced at his friends, trying to determine if they were truly interested in his day, or giving him a ride. They were good friends, old friends, but since the war he felt there had been something missing, something preventing his ability to fully reconnect. It was difficult being the only veteran in the bog. Of the three who volunteered to head south, he'd been the only one to return, and there were times he'd give anything to find the common bond he'd held during his year away. His hero's welcome had faded in a matter of weeks. The prestige of the job (created specifically for him) protecting the reconstructed school was gone in months. The badger chided him every morning about his layers of clothing. Deer looked down on him with disgust, always whispering within earshot (better to be a *farmer* . . . at least do *something* with his life). Something unspoken in Cal seemed to connect, but he was a dog of few words, and they rarely made it past pleasantries. Perhaps GW took himself too seriously. Every so often—over a few drinks—he told himself to move on. However, the resulting high from the day's adventure whispered otherwise.

"Well?" Hank raised his brow.

"*Well . . .?*" GW thought, wondering if it was worth it to risk ridicule tarnishing his tender pride. Today, he quickly decided, it was.

"I saved two lives today."

Hank shot to his feet. "No! Where?"

"In the Fells."

A sudden gasp from the table of frogs startled the room. GW looked around, seeing he had everyone's attention, and continued.

"It's true. In fact, I wrote a song on my walk here."

"You and your songs." Mildred's interest piqued. "Did you now?"

"He did not!" Hank clanged his thimble.

"I did."

160

One hand to his chest, the other to the air, the toad stood, licked his lips, and began to sing.

> *"The Woods has hosted the renown*
> *As our forefathers have told;*
> *But never a 'phibian, reptile, or fish*
>   *Compared with a Most Regal Toad!*
> *"The mammals to the north*

> *Know it is best to avoid the Fells.*
> *Since none of them possess one half the courage*
>   *As the veteran, GW Toad!*
> *"The pups fled from the school and cried,*
>   *Better to skip, than stay.*
> *Who was it said, 'Look out ahead!'*

> *The brave, GW Toad!*
> *"With harpoon slung over-shoulder*
> *Marched through the wood, and o'er the river.*
> *Was it Old Brown? Or the Badger? No.*

> *To the rescue, GW Toad!*
> *"The vermin, rat and weasel*
> *Brought the poor pups low.*
> *They threatened, 'Who's going to save you now?'*
> *Harpoons answered thrice, 'GW Toad.'"*

GW hesitated after the fifth verse—closed his eyes as he searched for the words. There was more to the song and more to be sung, but he'd only been able to memorize part (certainly proud of himself for recalling as much as he did on the spot), and so he concluded his performance with a short bow, raised his thimble, thanked his audience, and took a deep pull of grog.

"Bravo! Bravo!" Hank slapped his hands together, leading the applause. The female frog at the back whistled, swooning when GW acknowledged her with an innocent wink. Her date steamed at the interaction, popping their table with a fist, knocking over his thimble, spilling the last dribble of his drink.

"What a tale!" Mildred finished her grog. She held up the empty thimble, gesturing toward the bar. "Karly! Another round for the table, please."

"So much for the sipper," Hank quipped.

"Don't you get started, now." Mildred slapped him on the shell. "This is no time to get your shell all salty. We need to celebrate."

Karly delivered the next round herself, said, "On the house," and thanked GW with a hard squeeze on the shoulder. "The pups are great kids. They must have been so frightened—and fortunate to have you close by. What a catastrophe that might have been for the community."

GW gave a bit of an aw-shucks look, slightly blushing at the attention and praise. "I'm just glad I trusted my gut and was able to track and find them in time. It was too close, the more I think about it. If I hadn't gotten the drop on the rodents, it might have been a different story."

"Not when our favorite toad is on the job," Hank said. "For all the good-intentioned grief we give you, you've more than earned it. Cheers, brother."

GW tipped his drink back, basking in the glow of adoration, feeling as if he was finally receiving the respect he'd always deserved. "Wish I could have been there to witness the action," Hank said, finishing his sentence with a well-timed burp (and apologized for failing to cover his mouth).

"No, you don't. The Fells is not a nice place. Gave me the creeps the moment I crossed the river." GW felt a shiver run up his spine. "We stayed no longer than it took me to retrieve and wipe off a pair of harpoons."

"Why were the pups there in the first place?"

"I'm not sure. I overheard some of their whispers—about looking for their mother or father. I don't recall exactly, and I didn't press them on it. Cal dropped them off at school, but he wasn't there when we returned. They're off working on the decorations for the Moon Festival."

While the trio continued to discuss the day's events with great joy and interest, it was a very different story elsewhere. In the back of the pub, the male frog tossed back another thimble, growing visibly frustrated as he and his date watched the raucous celebration overtake the Drinkery. He finally called out to them to keep it down, and when no one, not even his date, acknowledged his voice, he hopped down from his seat and padded over to the trio.

"Hey!" he shouted as he approached, jabbing a webbed finger at GW. "You think you're some kind of big shot? That you can just come in here and sing and dance for our attention? Probably made it all up."

"Whoa there, friend," Mildred said, sticking out an arm in front of the frog, inching him backward. "Do you know who this is?"

"Uh, yeah. He only told me five times over the course of his 'song.'"

"This is Sir George Washington, a most regal toad," Hank instructed. "And you are?"

"Frog."

"Frog? Just Frog?" Mildred asked.

"No 'just'—Frog."

"What in the world . . ." Hank slapped his own forehead in disbelief. "Your parents run out of names?"

GW held up a hand and Hank quieted, backing down.

"I apologize if we impacted your evening. Please, let me buy you and your date a drink."

"Don't apologize to this wet blanket," Hank said, sitting up, rocking on the edge of his chair.

"Who're you calling wet blanket?" Frog asked, balling his webbed hands into fists.

Robinson stepped forward from the bar. "Excuse me, there's no need for—"

"Quiet, lizard. Who asked you—?"

Robinson grabbed Frog by the throat, slipped a leg behind him and tripped him to the ground. Frog struggled beneath him for a moment until it was clear he was trapped; the lizard was much stronger than him, even without the advantage of leverage.

"I'm feeling generous with the celebration tonight. This is your one warning. Take care of your lady and quit embarrassing yourself."

Frog aimed to protest, but Robinson shut him down. "Not another peep."

Frog reluctantly agreed, sucking on his tongue. Before Robinson could help him to his feet, the bell above the entry sang, pulling the room's attention to see the mask of a raccoon appear in the fading light. The ragamuffin took his time limping through the open door—the breeze sucked the warmth from the grotto. He shivered as he threw the door shut behind him, oblivious to the impact of his slow pace.

"Well, well, well," Maurice snickered, commenting on drama concluding on the floor. "Did I pick an interesting night to drop in? Or is it always like this? It's been so long since my last visit I've forgotten what sort of vibe to expect from this hole." He took the place in, perusing the decor. "The candles are a nice touch. I must say I'm jealous of their effect."

GW shot to his feet, eyeing his harpoon gun, which he'd hung on the wall beside the door. Maurice noticed the weapon and held his arms up in a gesture of peace.

"No need, friend. I'm just here to have a drink."

"Since when did your kind stop in just to have a drink?" Hank stood in support of GW, muttering, "I got your back against this *mammal*."

Karly interjected, "I warned you, Hank. I'm no fan of this filth—and that's what you are, *Maurice*—but we take all kinds here. As long as you can fit through that door, you are welcome. Got it?"

Hank waved her off, acknowledging his error as close to an apology as she would receive. It was true that the Drinkery rarely turned patrons away. Fights and worse were forgiven with an admission of guilt and demonstration of good behavior (after all, these were animals who erred savage on the best of days) and even the worst perpetrators were let back in eventually. The bog was host to its own crew of vermin—rats, and other fiends drawn to decay—but Maurice and the residents of the Fells were different, their scent unmistakable and threatening. The inhabitants of the bog knew of Maurice and his crew through story and song well before they laid eyes on the foreigners, if they ever did. Like those who found their home in the Woods, the boggies stayed away from the Fells, for even if the stories weren't true, they had most everything they required within reach, and there wasn't much to the north to interest them in the first place.

"Thank you for the *overwhelming* support, Miss." Maurice dipped forward, performing a weak bow. "I'm in no state to be looking for trouble."

Robinson pulled Frog to his feet, giving him a slight shove toward his table, out of the raccoon's path. Maurice limped to the bar and took a seat on a stool, back exposed to much of the room.

"Whew!" He wiped his brow, ordering a drink. "Feels good to take a load off these old feet. It is a long walk down here along the river. It's been so long I'd forgotten." He twisted on the stool to see most of the pub with his good eye. "Anyone in for another round?"

"I've had my fill," GW said, his voice full of disdain.

Only Frog raised a hand to take Maurice up on the offer. Karly ordered him to put it down. "You've had your fill as well. You'd be best not to tempt your good standing."

Maurice turned back to the bar and raised his thimble. "Well then. A toast to us all and our collective good health."

Karly nodded, left her place behind the bar to collect empties. A tense silence descended over the room.

After a few sips, Maurice sighed and put his drink down on the bar. "Don't let my presence ruin your night. I'm sure there was all sorts of lively discussion prior to my arrival. It appeared that way, at least." He looked to Robinson. "No?" The lizard stared straight ahead, arms behind his back—a silent sentry guarding his post. When Karly returned from clearing the frogs' table, he asked her how her family was doing.

"I've heard rumors of a sickness going around, making its way south. Awful stuff," he added.

"You haven't seen any dogs around, have you? Maybe Cal? Doubt his wife would come around here—no offense—but I suppose you never know. I'd hate to think they might be the source of all this, but I don't want to speak out of turn. Rumors and all that."

Karly shrugged as she wiped down the far end of the bar.

GW glanced around to find each animal in their own world, staring off in a random direction as if willing the raccoon to leave. How *dare* he spread ill rumors and tarnish the dogs' reputation? He thought of the pups and all they'd been through, the questions and attention they'd face in the coming days and weeks as the story spread and the truth fractured. He imagined snatching the harpoon gun from the wall and putting a bolt through the raccoon's back, pinning him to the bar. It left him both thrilled and disgusted with himself to fall from a heroic rescue to dreams of skullduggery and assassinations. This wasn't *war*. The longer he endured the silence, the more he felt trapped in his skin, heart thudding against his chest, afraid of what he might do if he were to speak up and the raccoon were to meet his challenge. He would not let this fiend ruin his night.

GW stood, pressing out the wrinkles in his vest, said, "I'm going for a walk."

Hank pushed back from the table, chair legs digging into the damp floor. "I'll join you. Mildred?"

The salamander swirled the contents of her thimble, gave them a half-hearted salute goodbye. "I'm going to finish my drink. I'll catch up with you two tomorrow."

"Give Mr. Robinson my regards," Hank whispered as he rounded the table, eliciting a hard slap on his shell from Mildred.

The tortoise donned his hat and left, waiting outside while GW put on his layers. First his belt with the quiver of harpoons. Then the snow pants and windbreaker. Next the scarf, wrapped neatly around his neck, and finally, the down winter coat. While in the process of slinging his harpoon gun over his shoulder, Maurice spoke up.

"Still keeping watch outside the school, toad?"

After a moment GW replied that, yes, in fact he was.

"A very important position these days. Don't ever let anyone tell you otherwise. I don't believe everything I hear, but where there's smoke . . .," he trailed off. "There's little worse than a sick little one struggling to fight for another day."

GW finished zipping the coat up to his chin. The pub was too warm for him to pull over the hood, and he felt himself beginning to perspire, the tang of grog wafting up. The raccoon looked at him with his good eye, and GW returned his stare and left without another word.

Once outside he wished he'd thanked Karly, or at least said farewell. For, as down as the evening concluded, she'd helped bring his celebration to life.

Hank sat on one of several small rocks near the entrance, a thin trail of smoke drifting upwards from a pipe in his mouth. Behind him, the setting sun set the horizon ablaze, its red-orange hue peeking between clouds in the darkening sky.

"What was that all about?"

"I don't know and I don't like it." GW shook his head. "Shouldn't be coming down here and stirring up mud. I'm half-tempted to order him out and shoo him back north."

"You want to go through with it, I got your back." Hank stood and put an arm around GW's shoulders as they walked along the path toward home.

"I'm afraid I've had enough excitement for one day."

"You should write another song about this."

"Not when it's unfinished business. It's nothing I'd enjoy singing."

"That lady frog was pretty cute, by the way."

"Stop it."

"What? Toads and frogs can't mix?"

"Don't get me all worked up, now."

The two friends had a good laugh, venturing home to the tune of jangling harpoons under the setting sun.

* * *

Maurice left the Drinkery hiding his frustration amid the pain of his limp. His early-morning decision that a short stay and a couple of drinks was worth the journey baffled him. Perhaps it was the lack of sleep, or that the sickness had him more on edge than he'd like to admit. He dreaded the long walk home to the Fells, resisting the pull to find a good pile of leaves and call it a night. It wouldn't do to leave his crew unsupervised overnight with too much time to ponder where he'd gone, and if he was coming back. Plus, there was Clem to think of. He'd left his cousin alone for too long, though perhaps time—he hoped—was exactly what she needed to feel better. He'd come to the bog seeking information about the infection and found none. But the long day wasn't a total bust—he'd been able to tarnish Cal's reputation. Even though no one spoke up, he could tell they were considering his words. One way or another, it was past time he let Cal feel the sting of their years apart. He was too old, too fragile to let it go any longer.

Not far from the Drinkery, Maurice paused to lean on a tree

and look back over his shoulder. He could have sworn he heard the wind carrying the words of someone calling for him. He stuck a claw in his right ear and rummaged around, clearing the passage.

"Hey, wait up!" It was the salamander who'd been sitting with the toad and tortoise. Her eyes followed him as he settled up and left the pub. He'd found her interest odd, chalking it up as anger in support of her friends, wondering if she'd remained behind to keep tabs on him and ensure that he found his way out of the bog. She pursued him now, hands stuffed in the pockets of her velvet jacket. She looked about, her focus more on her surroundings than Maurice, running every few steps in a hurry to catch up. It was clear she was anxious and it set him on edge. When she drew near, she glanced behind her, nodded, gesturing to her right, and said, "Let's get off the path."

Maurice wasn't known to take direction well or without resistance. Weary, he followed the salamander a good distance off the path and behind a cluster of fallen trees. He was slow and she hurriedly waved him on, shivering with impatience.

"Come on then. I don't have all night."

Maurice ignored the quip, making an effort to present his best manners. "To whom do I owe the honor?"

"Name's not important. I know who you are though. You're that raccoon that haunts the Fells."

Haunt. Now, that's one he hadn't heard. He liked the ring of that— *haunt.* "Guilty, I suppose. I must say you've caught me by surprise. Your friends did not take to me well."

"That doesn't mean I have, either. You have quite the reputation around here and none of it in good standing. You're lucky the Drinkery was quiet—and my friends, the honorable, reluctant sort."

"Then I must ask, why are we here? I have a long walk ahead of me, and while I find comfort in the dark, I'm not fond of the coming chill."

"Of course. It's nearly winter and you're dressed for late spring."

"Then perhaps I'll take the jacket off the next boggie I see and warm up."

He grinned at her, exposing his ugly teeth, and she gasped, taking a step backward.

"Relax, I only kid. Don't expect me to stand here and weather your harsh criticism without a barb or two back."

The salamander swallowed hard, took a moment to compose herself, and continued.

"I've heard about the dogs' whereabouts and whatnot today."

"Yes? You've seen them?"

"Not me. A friend."

"Why not speak up in the pub? Why now?"

"It wasn't my story to tell then, but I've got a family and friends who live close by, near the Woods' border. If what you say is true about this sickness . . . we don't need any of that coming near the bog. I don't trust you, raccoon. But I need your word, and something in return."

"Trust is rarely a requirement. I say mutual interest is always better common ground—less likely to cause issues down the road. But go ahead with your terms then, salamander."

"Root out this sickness and keep you and your mammal friends away from the bog. You seem sharp, and might guess who of my associates is involved in what I'm about to tell you. You keep away from them as well."

"Vague and puzzling seeing as I know nothing of what you are about to share, but I'll agree to it. We are, after all, pursuing the same goal of keeping those close to us safe."

The salamander looked around again before beginning her tale. She told him of her friend's encounter with the pups in the Fells, the rescue and fight that left two of his dead. Which, given the circumstances, he was thankful for, as he was in no shape to return home only to discover he was at war with a cunning dog who'd just lost his boys. The last bit puzzled him as it wasn't entirely clear to the salamander, but the pups were either after their mother or father, one or both having gone into the Fells. Was it true that Winifred was sick and wandering the Fells? His patrols in danger of infection or worse? Had Cal gone in search of her? Or him? He'd seen enough smoke to believe there was fire. So many interesting possibilities to contemplate on his way home. He needed time. The more the salamander spoke, the more the long walk didn't look so unpleasant after all.

"Hello? You in there?"

He felt the poke of a stick against his chest and realized he'd been lost in thought, the salamander trying to get his attention.

"My apologies. You've given me a lot to think about."

The salamander backed away, deeper into the marshy woods. "Don't forget our deal."

"Of course. You won't catch a glimpse of me until our little problem is well past us." *That toad, however*, he thought, recalling the harpoons he'd slung over his back. He wouldn't be forgetting that, or his dead mates (however fortunate the circumstances) anytime soon. He gave the salamander a slight bow, and when he lifted his head, he found himself alone, darkness shrouding the world around him. His stomach rumbled—a reminder that grog, no matter how much one tipped back, was not a replacement for dinner. He snapped a thin limb from one of the nearby fallen logs. It was mostly dry and free of rot, and as his eyes adjusted to the evening, he nibbled at the end attempting to trick his belly into thinking food was on the way. It worked for the moment, though he knew it wouldn't last. The area around the bridge saw enough traffic that he was confident he'd come across something discarded to satisfy his hunger. One animal's trash is another animal's treasure. Carefully, he found his way back to the path, and headed toward home.

11

Maurice's scarred hip throbbed, a warm jolt of pain washing across his pelvis and down his leg with every beat of his heart. He'd traded his chew toy for a longer walking stick, and it helped, but not enough. Though he could see well in the dark, the foreign territory made it difficult to retrace his steps, slowing his pace to a crawl. He'd become so fixated on the salamander's words that he had to stop for a minute and reorient himself to prevent getting lost. The need to focus on his route home became the source of his frustration. There were big decisions to be made, and he needed his wits about him. The information the salamander provided refused to settle. Maurice trafficked in rumor—his crew—a lot of gossipers, tattletales, and backstabbers, but he wasn't sure what to think of it all, yet. But why was she (or Cal) in the Fells? Did she become ill on his watch? If she caught what Clem had, it couldn't be good. In fact, it could be very bad. He didn't want to overreact, but it would be prudent to pull his patrols back and wait for the infection to run its course and blow over. Clem was small enough to control, but Winifred would be another story.

As Maurice made his way east, the falling temperature clashed with the warmer bog air, creating a swirling mist along the ground that reminded him of the steam that rose off the Rubbish Heap during the winter months. After what felt like an hour had passed, he saw the torch-lit bridge crossing in the distance. His stomach gurgled—an angry reminder to check the reeds for anything that could pass for a meal. He prodded the thick overgrowth on either side of the bridge with his walking stick. His meager curiosity was rewarded with a brown husk of an apple core and a moldy cap of bread. His jaws overflowed with saliva at the sight, and he quickly polished off both—stem, seeds, and mold included— and returned to look for more. The second search took longer, but again he was rewarded, uncovering a soggy brown bag full of peanut shells. He cursed as the bag shredded upon retrieval and spilled most of its contents at his feet. He clenched his teeth, willing himself through the pain of crouching down to retrieve the fallen dessert. Lifting a handful of muddy shells, he froze, mouth agape. He sniffed the air.

Peanuts and . . .

The sound of footsteps on the bridge all but confirmed his suspicions, and he chuckled to himself at the surreal moment. His face full of peanut shells, Maurice looked up to witness Cal emerge from the gloom, feet thumping on the wooden bridge. Cal remained on the bridge, bracing his elbows atop the railing, eyes locked on Maurice's kneeling figure. Torch light flickered across his form, lending him a twisted, veiled look. If not for the soft creaking of the bridge, the shadowy figure could have passed for a revenant come to stalk Maurice's every move. Maurice shuddered at the thought. His hearing seemed to worsen with the passing of each season, and he squeezed his good eye shut and then open to ensure the figure really was Cal (it was), and not some figment of his imagination. Maurice groped blindly along the ground for another handful, this time more weeds and mud than shells. He grimaced at the sludge and then choked it down before loosing a loud, acid-lined belch.

"Come all this way for a drink?" Cal wrinkled his nose.

"Why else visit the bog?" Maurice held up the savaged bag of peanuts. "The food here is decidedly terrible."

"Well, you *are* eating bog mud." He shuffled across the bridge toward Maurice. "I suppose a drink or two is reason enough for a visit. But leaving so soon? It's quite the hike from the Rubbish Heap. If my legs are sore, I can't imagine how your feet are holding up with that limp. Why don't you stick around? We'll chat, have a few laughs."

"I've learned it's better to leave while you're ahead than to overstay your welcome."

Maurice tried to stand but the pain in his hip overwhelmed him and he knelt back down. "It reeks of tragic desperation, doesn't it? The air around us is full of the stench. Look at us—me on my claws and knees like some pauper. And you—" Maurice squished his claws together, squeezing a glop of mud "an enigma of bottled-up emotions, standing there like you always have, above it all. There was always that whiff about you, that you thought you were better than us."

Cal grinned, his sharp canines slick in the fire light. "How introspective. I don't recall you giving much thought to your surroundings."

"Your need for a confidant was always a weakness." With his claw, Maurice traced a circle around his right ear. "I had little choice other than to let these marbles rattle around. If only you knew what it felt like to be betrayed by those closest to you." He licked his lips, sneering as he swiped the last of the muck from the corners of his mouth. "How I yearn for you to have that bitter taste. It has a habit of lingering for *years*."

Maurice clutched his walking stick, stabbed it into the mud, and forced himself up with a harsh grunt. He turned and tried to move past Cal, but the dog stepped forward into his way.

"Is that right? What prevents you from packing up and walking away? Afraid your crew will come for you while you sleep? Drag you out from beneath a bed of leaves and devour you, bite after little bite?"

"Unlike you, I know my place in this game. I'm not a bad guy, Cal. You Woods folk look up to Old Brown like he's some omni potent spirit watching over your world. *Pathetic*. Where was he during the fire? Where is he when winter strikes early and animals are ragged and starving?"

"He keeps the Fells in check."

Maurice laughed. "He comes down from his throne when he's *bored*. I am the dam that holds back the Rubbish Heap from devouring your precious Woods. I am the one who herds the hungry mouths of ever-multiplying vermin. I am your savior,

Cal." Tears trickled down the raccoon's face as he trembled. "You were lost and I gave you a home, protection, and order for a naive pup. Even after you abandoned us I resisted, holding those back who cried for your pelt. Imagine your life in this world when I am gone."

Cal barked a hard, fake laugh in Maurice's face. "*My savior?* You are mad with too many years cooped up inside that empty head, alone with your thoughts. Nearly ten years without a word and you show up in the dead of night with vague threats, questioning the whereabouts of my wife. Rumors abound of infection. And now you're here, *alone*. What are you up to?"

Maurice swallowed hard, looking at Cal, then away, and back again as the salamander's words tumbled through his head. He sensed the rage burning in his old friend. He needed to say something to deflect, to calm. He needed time, the time he was supposed to have alone on his walk home

Alone. The word echoed in his ears as he stared at Cal. He was alone.

Fear gripped Maurice by the throat, a first in a very long time. An emotion he'd fought tooth and claw to suppress when among his crew. It carried an unmistakable odor, screamed weakness, and bloomed wicked power struggles. He saw Cal's nose twitch and knew he'd been made. He tried to back up and stumbled. Cal caught him by a pawful of chest fur, driving him backward into an old birch tree, slamming his head into its papery bark. He growled, snapping his jaws an inch from Cal's face.

"Answer me!" Cal slammed him into the tree again. Maurice's vision blurred, and he felt a small cut open on the back of his head. "What happened to my wife? Answer me now, damn it!"

Maurice tried to speak, to find the word—any word—but his voice had fled. He made a weak attempt to push Cal away as he was pulled forward for another slam. Cal was answered by the cry of a hawk, instead, and he felt a flap of wings and a strong gust of wind as one of Maurice's birds flew low in a dive over the bridge. A scream followed as the hawk released something from its grasp. A small animal hit the ground hard, its limbs flopping as it rolled over and over toward Cal and Maurice. While Cal held Maurice firm to the tree, the pair looked down to see a bloodied rat, bandage tight across its chest, its legs mangled—bone exposed, and clearly broken. It opened its eyes, blinked several times in shock, and coughed through a hoarse scream as it tried to lift its right arm and found it limp, dislocated at the shoulder. It took a deep breath, looked up to see Cal, and screamed again. The wretched sound jolted Maurice with a shot of adrenaline. Between the darkness and his poor vision, he didn't recognize the vermin (who could blame him with the number of rats running around the Rubbish Heap on any given night) so he barked "Rat!" at him a few times until he calmed down.

"Boss!" the rat's voice no louder than a whisper, face contorted in anguish with each word. "Boss!"

Maurice gasped. "Jefferson? Is that you?"

"Yes!"

"What is this? Your backup?" Cal said, sneering in disgust at the fallen rodent. When Maurice didn't answer, he shook him hard, said, "Well?"

"He's a messenger, you nitwit. Do you not remember? Have you locked away all of your memories of our years together?"

"Unfortunately, I have not, though this . . . practice must have been after my time. What good is a messenger if they end up like this?"

"There are some kinks to work out. The hawks are supposed to drop them low, into water or a bush to soften the landing. Their accuracy, especially at night, is . . . lacking, at best." Maurice lowered his voice to a whisper. "Though this outcome does make for a nice one-time use without worry of capture or desertion. I'm overwhelmed with volunteers eager to experience flight and give it a shot."

"Boss!" the rat interrupted. He'd closed his eyes, dropped his head back to the ground.

"Out with it, Jefferson!"

"But . . . it's for you alone."

Cal flexed his grip on Maurice, pinching his fur. "I'm not leaving."

Jefferson began to speak anyway, but Maurice shook his head. Keeping his left paw low, he waved to get the rat's attention, then wiggled two claws to imitate a creature running, hoping he'd catch his instruction to perform the message in code. To his shock, he did.

Slow and purposeful, Jefferson lifted his good arm and pointed to a bandage wrapped around his mid-section. He raised his arm then and opened his claws outward from a fist, demonstrating something rising from below, and scratched at the air. Then he opened his mouth to show his teeth and bit down.

Maurice's good eye drew wide, the fear he'd felt in front of Cal growing two-fold. The rat could only be communicating one thing: Clem had escaped.

"Hurry," Jefferson managed to squeak, before collapsing with a heavy sigh, and succumbing to the pain, or death.

Maurice shook, his legs threatening to buckle as he processed the dying rat's message. Aside from Jefferson, he had told no one of what he'd hidden in the bowels of the Rubbish Heap, and now he had unleashed her upon them. He'd meant well, but it was a mistake to lock her away. He'd known it even as he locked the shackles over her thin wrists. There was always the possibility of her escape, but it was in everyone's best interest to keep her away, give her time to heal and beat the infection. He'd never planned to be away this long. Mistake after mistake, after mistake, after mistake—

Cal slapped him hard across the face. The action sent Maurice's head swirling, his vision twinkling with stars. Maurice managed to keep his head up, only to receive another harsh slap. The left side of his face stung, his upper lip cracked and bleeding.

Cal clenched his free paw into a fist. "How dare you communicate in code. I should rip out your innards and string them across the bridge."

"Why don't you ask the rat himself?"

Cal took a step back and slugged Maurice in the stomach. Maurice doubled over, crashing to his knees, expelling a mouthful of half-digested mud. Somehow it tasted better coming up than it had going down.

Cal left him and crouched down beside the rat, placing a paw gently over the rat's chest.

"Maybe I will. This one appears to possess a strong desire to survive—he still breathes."

"Not for long."

"That so? Then maybe I'll settle for my first option." Maurice clawed at the dirt, stretching for his walking stick just out of reach. He gave up as Cal approached, and pushed himself backward into the tree. He raised his claws and hissed through clenched teeth, preparing for his final stand.

On your rump in the dark, covered in mud and bile. What a depressing way to go.

Cal paused a foot away from Maurice, head cocked, listening, eyes on the dark sky.

That's it! You're *the one who's afraid, aren't you, dog*, Maurice thought. *You should be. A desperate, cornered animal is a savage that one does not take lightly.*

Then the voices in Maurice's head quieted long enough for him to hear it too, and he realized Cal's delay had nothing to do with him. A bell clanged in the distance, hard, back and forth, over and over, ringing with reckless abandon. Maurice knew immediately it had to be Clem. He had to get back to the Fells and check on the Heap. With strength he had no idea he possessed, Maurice pressed his back into the tree, pushing against it to force himself to his feet. Power flooded his veins, his aging body invigorated with a youthful strength, his limbs moving so fast his mind could barely keep up, as if he was on escape auto-pilot. Before Cal could react, he'd snatched his walking stick with one claw, grabbed Jefferson with the other, and ran for the bridge, making it all the way across before looking back to see that Cal had vanished. Numb to the pain, Maurice ran north, hobbling as fast as his legs could carry him, into the dark.

* * *

Cal thought of his pups as the bell continued to ring, wondering where they were and if they were okay. He'd been so focused on Winifred and Maurice that he neglected to even attempt to pick them up from school. Billiam surely took them again; there was more than another evening's work to spend on the Moon Festival. Still, he felt guilty and hoped with every ounce of his being that the emergency had nothing to do with them.

Bark flaked from the birch tree as Maurice pushed himself upright. Mouth open, one eye wide, the raccoon sucked wind as he moved past Cal, his joints cracking as he bent low to grab a stick and a few steps later the rat, along with a clump of mud. He moved in slow motion, as if his lower body was traveling through a river of molasses. Cal could have stuck out a leg and tripped him, or tackled him with little effort, but he let him go.

He'd spent too much of the day chasing ghosts. Now that he was presented with a real emergency, his path was clear. He left Maurice as the raccoon hit the bridge, nearly tripping on his face, and headed north to the Woods and the unknown.

12

EARLIER

Duchess tapped out a rhythm on the counter with her left paw, patiently (ever so patiently) waiting for the next customer to arrive. An old hymn about the scent of wild flowers and sunny countryside days had been stuck in her head since she'd woken in the early-morning hours to dress and make her short walk to the store. The hedgehog had inherited the old general store from her mother (rest her soul) and done her best to keep it in tip-top shape. Each day she dressed in uniform—one of several frilly dresses with a matching lace bow tied beneath her chin, and a white apron with pink polka dots around her waist. The apron had been patched, sewn, and passed down for generations. "If you want respect, you have to dress for it," her mother was fond of saying, "especially for those tradesmen who'd rather see us starve than offer a fair price." Duchess had never met such a passing tradesman, figuring perhaps her mother, and her mother before her, had established a tone that they were not to be toyed with when it came to haggling. The hardships her ancestors had suffered for her benefit were not lost on her.

Early foot traffic had been slow, becoming virtually non-existent after the lunch hour—as it had all week after word of her bare shelves got around. She'd already dusted and reorganized the remnants of her goods enough times to drive her mad, settling on spreading them out to make her stock appear better than it was. The damned caravan was three days late with her supplies. She wasn't one to put too much weight in worries (as the lone shopkeeper in the Woods, there wasn't too much to be concerned about), but the cats who ran the route had never missed a date, even in their graying years. The previous day, when Helen bought the last sack of flour (and gave Duchess more grief over the lacking setup than a pig had the right to—the nerve of her to ask if Duchess was closing shop!) Duchess made the decision to take matters into her own hands. She'd prepared to spend the following night nestled behind the counter at the shop in case the cats ventured into the Woods late. Along with her lunch she'd packed a light dinner fare and a thermos of milk. She'd rolled the items in a blanket to which she'd strapped a pillow with some twine. It was a bit much to carry, but the walk was short and she managed with the roll slung over her shoulders. If the night proved uneventful and they failed to show, she was determined to go off and find them on her own. The idea of venturing far outside of the Woods filled her with fright (she'd never been more than a two-hour's trek from the shop), but she knew the cats would enter the Woods from the trading route due east across the bridge, and it couldn't hurt to give it a half-a-day's journey. What's the worst that could happen?

You could lose your way, she reminded herself. There could be a break-in at the shop (for what? a pinch of stale barley?). She'd written out a full list of potential poor outcomes—leaving off death, as her relatives all lived to a ripe old age and it was the furthest thing from her mind. The health and success of the general store outweighed all the negative outcomes. After all, her existence and sense of self was tied directly to the building, and if it were to fall apart under her watch, where would that leave her?

"Impossible," she said aloud. The store had survived far worse than a missing shipment. This was just a test.

Duchess finished tapping out the tune for the umpteenth time when the door opened to reveal Sly Frances, creaky red wagon in tow. She wore a light-green turtleneck sweater with a multi-color plaid scarf wrapped loosely around her neck and shoulders. The fox made her home beneath an old oak tree on the southwest edge of the Woods, a site of much development and experimentation. Throughout history foxes earned a reputation for thievery, but Frances was quite the opposite—giving instead of taking, forcing her inventions on the Woods folk and beyond. If one didn't know her, one might mistake her sales tactics for typical guile—a traveling snake oil saleswoman selling intense fragrances guaranteed to find you love, or fortified breads that strengthened muscle and bone—except Frances truly believed in all her creations (even if they only sometimes worked). She wore hope on her sleeve, her fingers forever crossed.

"Speaking of tests . . ." Duchess muttered. "Hullo, Frances."

"Hullo, Duchess! I believe I have the solution to your woes."

"Is that right? If so, count me shocked—I believe that would be a first."

"Now, there's no time for rude talk. Look at these bare shelves!"

"Nothing to worry about. A shipment is on the way."

Frances struggled with the weight of the wagon, balancing the contents while squeezing it through the entrance and lifting the front wheels over the lip. "And it's right here," Frances said, taking the wagon by the handle and pulling it the remainder of the way into the store. As the fox wheeled it across the checkered floor, Duchess saw the wagon was full of small packages that looked like cakes or cheeses wrapped in wax paper and tied with rough twine. When she reached the counter, Frances selected one from the top of the pile and dropped it in front of Duchess, the parcel landing with a hard thud.

"Heavy," Duchess said, picking it up. "What is it?"

"May I present to you, my dear Duchess, my finest mud oat cakes."

Duchess sniffed at the package. "Smells like sweet mud."

"True to its name. I used a bit of mud as a binding agent, along with some flour, sugar, and a smattering of secret ingredients, cinnamon being one. Go ahead and try some. I brought enough for you to divvy up for customers to sample."

"I don't know . . . I'd hate to spoil my supper."

"One bite can't hurt—though I must say they are quite addicting. You might find it difficult to put a cake down after a nibble."

A knock at the door interrupted Frances's sales pitch. Duchess cupped her paws around her mouth and called out for the customer to come in. "No need to knock! We're open." She put heavy emphasis on the word, the knock eliciting renewed paranoia over the future of her business. Does everyone think the shop is on the verge of closing? Where would everyone go? Too many hours alone filled her head with silly thoughts. There were two potential buyers in her store at the same time. This could be the moment her week turned around for the better.

Billiam entered the shop, stopping to wipe his feet on the entry mat. He held a large, lumpy sack slung over his left shoulder. "Good evening, ladies."

Frances let out a long sigh at the sight of him.

"I heard that. You should be worried, but I'll get to you in a minute, huckster, after I peruse the fine goods of this establishment." The badger walked around the perimeter of the store, eyeing the newly arranged shelves.

"Spare me your false praise." Duchess frowned, hopes of a sale quickly dashed.

Billiam feigned insult. "Me? I'd never. Look at this place—so clean, organized and—"

"Empty. The shipment is still in the wind."

"*What*?" Billiam gasped as he approached the counter. "The success of the Moon Festival is riding on those damn cats and their stubborn mule."

"It's a moose," Frances corrected him. "His name's Buford."

"Whatever. Doesn't change the fact that they're late. Unacceptable."

Duchess crossed her arms over her chest. "Tell me about it."

"Next thing you know, I'll be scraping bark off the trees and boiling it for supper like I'm half-deer." The badger shivered, muttering to himself, "Eating raw bark straight off the tree . . . savages."

"I baked mud oat cakes," Frances said, selecting one from her wagon. "Here, have a go."

Billiam recoiled in disgust. "Fool me once, fox . . ." He pulled the sack off his shoulder, sat it down hard on the counter in front of Duchess. A roughly sewn patch popped off the side, acorns spilling from the hole.

"Candied acorns!" Frances snatched one from the pile and popped it in her mouth, teeth crunching down on the morsel. Her face twitched, body following suit with a shudder. "Woo, these are strong."

"Strong? That's what I call spoiled. These acorns are so bitter I spit them out. You expect me to serve these at the festival?"

"Acorns *are* bitter."

"Not the batch I ordered."

Duchess gave the acorns a sniff. She stood up quickly, wafting the scent away, her eyes watering. "A whole one of those and I fear I'd be staggering home."

Frances selected another from the counter. "These look to be extra-candied. Did I make them?"

Billiam nodded, looking down his nose at the two before him. "And I want a refund."

Frances thought for a moment, said, "I haven't whipped up a batch since last autumn. These are over a year old. No wonder they are so strong.

"Duchess, might you have a bit of paper I can borrow? I suspect aged candied acorns will be the next big hit!"

The hedgehog dug into the pouch of her apron and produced a scrap and pencil. Frances thanked her and went to work, jotting down a flurry of notes.

"Are either of you listening to me? These are unacceptable." Billiam steamed, stomped his foot. "As your sole elected official, I demand something be done to rectify the situation post-haste!"

"One moment, friend," Frances said, continuing to scribble away. "Thoughts are fleeting, especially when it comes to ideas for new recipes. I've forgotten more than I care to remember."

Billiam snatched the fox's arm at the elbow. "The Moon Festival is less than a week away. The tables and chairs are soaked. The field is a muddy mess. I'm low on supplies. There's no food, and I've left the kids unsupervised, probably wrapping each other in streamers or whatever nonsense they do when no adults are around, to come here and resolve this matter."

"Are you quite done?"

"And it's cold."

"Good. Now get your paws off me this instant." Frances snarled at Billiam and he let go, taking a step back.

Duchess cleared her throat and pointed to a well-worn list of rules and regulations tacked behind the counter. "You know my policy is not to accept any sort of return after a month, especially when it comes to perishable food. Imagine if I allowed such a thing? Half the Woods would be in here all willy-nilly with this or that complaint.

"*However*, I understand the pressure you face. The festival is the highlight of the year for many in the Woods, and I've done you no favors with my bare cupboard.

"I'll make you a deal. If what Frances says is true—and this much I believe—these acorns are over a year old, and well outside my policy."

Billiam made a harrumph sound, placing his paws on his hips, a look of consternation on his face.

"But if you can produce a bill of sale or a receipt of your purchase, I will exchange your acorns when the next shipment arrives."

"A *receipt* . . ." Billiam muttered through clenched teeth, staring at the hedgehog. He looked away then, as if pondering the offer.

"A generous offer if I ever heard one," added Frances.

"Quiet, you. This all started because of whatever corners you cut in your preparation of this rubbish."

"Now—," the fox tried to defend her methods but Billiam continued, cutting her off.

"As the sole elected official of the Woods and organizer of the annual Moon Festival—among other events—I'll have you know I keep immaculate records. While I find your offer unfair, I will head straight home to find the receipt in question and return this evening to put this matter to rest." He extended a paw and shook with the hedgehog, sealing the deal.

"That was something," Frances quipped. "Don't call me in as a witness when things go south."

Billiam snatched one of the mud oat cakes from France's wagon, and said, "I'm taking one of these."

"Thief," she muttered to his back as he turned to leave.

"Takes one to know one, *fox*."

Billiam took a bite of the cake as he opened the door. He turned back as he exited to shout, "Your mud cakes suck!" taking a second bite before disappearing, leaving the door open in his wake.

Duchess sighed and wiped her brow. What a day she'd had— uneventful, and yet stressful all the same. And, she wasn't done yet—she needed to remain semi-alert overnight in case the caravan showed. Maybe she'd close up and go home. It would not do to spend tomorrow exhausted, especially if she continued with her plan to go in search of the old cats.

"So, about my cakes . . ."

Duchess snapped to attention. "Right, sorry. Where were we?"

"You were about to sample my latest mud oat cakes and purchase the wagon-load for the store."

"I don't know, Frances . . . aren't these just mud?"

"Mud is an ingredient, but they're so much more! We could change the name if you'd like—I was just going for a play on the mud pies we'd made as kids. Have a taste."

"I'll take Billiam's word for it, or actions, rather."

"He did take a liking to it, didn't he?" Frances said with a wry smile. "Felt quite pleased with myself in that moment."

The two haggled over quantity and price, with Duchess taking on more than she would have liked, as was custom when going at it with Frances. Exhaustion took its toll, the stresses of the week piling up, making her not her usual self, cutting to the chase more quickly than she'd have liked. In the end, she took half the cakes, with a commitment to more if they sold, in exchange for store credit. Frances wasn't entirely pleased with the deal, but Duchess couldn't recall a time when she'd been any other way. "As an inventor and traveling sales-fox," she'd once said, "I'm never satisfied. There's always something new to discover, a better deal to be made."

After unloading the cakes onto the counter, the two said their goodbyes, and Frances turned her wagon around and took her leave.

At the door she asked, "Would you like the door left propped open? It felt a bit stuffy toward the back of the shop."

"Please. What a fine idea. I could use the air, thank you."

Once the fox was gone, Duchess pulled her thermos from underneath the counter, and poured herself a cap-full of milk. She drained the cap and poured herself another and set it on the counter beside the thermos to sip on while she inventoried the parcels.

"Might as well place you at the front," she said, grabbing an armful from the counter. The fact that they were new trumped whether they were actually good, and with the current stigma, they needed to be front and center if they were to draw in the passing eye. She crouched down at one of the front endcaps that had been empty for weeks. She dumped the cakes to the floor and began to stack them one by one, spreading them out to take up space like she'd done with the rest of her shop. Half-way through the work, she found herself feeling hungry and set aside one of the smaller squares for herself. She was tempted to tear off the wrapping and dig in, but decided it would do her some good to wait and relax with a little dessert after she closed up.

If Duchess had tasted the cake right then and there, she would have found it so irresistibly scrumptious that she would have run to the back and made note to order more. But as the shadow descended over her through the open door, all she could think about was why she had taken so many mud oat cakes, and how—given the current circumstances—they might be the death of her.

Billiam whistled on his way back to the general store, so pleased with himself he could almost skip (if not for his status as the sole elected official of the Woods and his need to maintain a modest, professional look when in public). He gave the breast pocket of his jacket a tap, feeling the paper receipt crinkle behind the thin fabric. As promised, he'd marched straight home, ducking past the missus and the twins ("Daddy has very important business to attend to!") to his office. The last three months of work was spilled haphazardly across every surface, including the floor, as life with three young ones slowly closed its death grip on his ability to hold everything together. The worse it got, the more he avoided the room, only entering to shuffle papers around to stack more.

But—and a very important *but*—anything older than last quarter's downward spiral was filed neatly by category and date within one of three filing cabinets beside his desk (or what used to function as a desk). In a matter of minutes, he'd tiptoed across the room, found the correct drawer, file, and receipt for the candied acorns. Unable to contain his excitement he'd rushed from the office, toppling stacks of he could-only-guess what, gave the missus a kiss and the kids a quick pat, and left with "I'll be back after the—," cutting himself off with the slam of the front door. He cringed, opened the door a crack to apologize and finish "after the kids are done working on the festival, love you, bye!", pulled the door snug, and was on his way.

The sun had set by the time he reached the shop, but Duchess usually stayed late, and besides, the door was open so he felt good—mission accomplished. He took out the receipt from his pocket as he approached, noticing the cakes, some stacked and others on the floor, and scoffed at Duchess for dealing with Frances. The treat was quite good, but it burned him to see the sly fox do well. He could barely get his constituents to agree on anything, while she could sell bottled bog water to a frog.

It wasn't until he'd set foot in the doorway that he noticed the blood spatter among the fallen desserts. The receipt slipped from his paw, coming to rest on the sticky floor, an afterthought. His body tensed—claws up, teeth bared—as fight-or-flight instincts calculated, pumping hormones through his system.

A bloody trail of struggle led toward the back, where shelving was knocked to the floor and its contents spilled across the room. He took one step inside, then another, and yelled, "Duchess!" as he made his way toward the counter. When he heard nothing he ran, calling out for her again, and again, until he reached the counter and the words caught in his throat. He found her—what was left of her—slumped against the wall. Duchess, murdered—not just murdered, savaged. Billiam placed a paw on the counter to steady himself, found it slick with blood.

Who could have done this? Frances? He pictured the fox arguing with the hedgehog after he left. The sale wasn't going well and things escalated too quickly, and then—.

An imagined attack played out in his head, and in his adrenaline-fueled state, he convinced himself she was the culprit. He then turned his focus on himself. He was the last one to see them together, to see Duchess alive. Frances knew he'd be coming back, knew he could connect her to the scene. Knew—

He dry heaved, took a deep breath to compose himself, took one last look, and bolted for the exit. Throwing caution to the wind, he ran for the warning bell that hung fifty yards from the store. Billiam had never moved so fast in his life. His lungs sucked wind, arms pumping, carrying him across the finish line, and crashing into the post.

He grabbed the rope attached to the bell and pulled hard, again and again, until his ears rang and all thought scattered from his mind.

13

Cal crouched beside Duchess's remains in the back of the general store, a borrowed handkerchief pressed over his nose and mouth in a poor attempt to stifle the gamy scent of blood and death. Neither smell particularly offended him, per se, but given the situation (and potential prying eyes) he felt it played well to display some weakness at the sight of her contorted body. Most of the curious crowd had stomped their way through the scene for a good look, and now stood outside pale and shaken, clutching their children, gossiping their way to ready-made conclusions. Billiam insisted he not dawdle near the body. Everyone who set foot inside the General Store sensed something was off, a scent of disease that lingered beyond death. Gossip spread of a plague upon the Woods. While it was only whispers, it made Cal deeply worried.

At some point, a well-intentioned animal had cut a burlap sack into a sheet and laid it over the body. Unfortunately, gore had soaked through the makeshift cover in several spots, forming a thick glue-like adhesive, and forcing Cal to place a paw on Duchess's shoulder to hold the body down and peel it off. Immediately he understood why others felt ill at the sight of her. Duchess was a mess—her throat ravaged, small bites had torn chunks from her arms, her apron ripped away, the contents of her insides splayed about, as if something had rooted around, unable to find what they were looking for despite having full access. Whoever— *whatever*—had attacked her had been out of control. *Or had wanted to appear that way . . .*

The scene reminded him of a particularly lean winter at the Rubbish Heap, when one of his roaming packs of vermin stumbled upon an otter who'd strayed from the river into the Fells and become trapped in a pitfall. Instead of neatly killing the otter for his fur, they'd descended into the hole as one, savagely tearing the otter limb from limb. When Cal had caught up to check on them, he discovered the gruesome sight within the hole, the gang and their victim barely recognizable.

Everything behind the counter had been destroyed, tossed, or violently altered in some way. A bloodied pillow sat spilling feathers in the corner. A shredded paper bag, bread crumbs and bits of twine lay beside the body, along with a severely dented thermos, as if the attacker had first tried smashing it open before figuring out how to work the cap. Cal picked up on notes of stinky cheese and milk. Something heavy had been pulled up and over the counter, leaving behind a streak of blood, but the rest of the scene was too trampled with footprints for him to tell what it was, or where it might have gone. Or who took it, for that matter.

It appeared Duchess had put up a good fight—if the wake of the struggle across the checkered floor was any indication. Her claws were streaked with blood and there were bits of grayish-white fur under her nails and clumped beside her that could only belong to her killer. He stood and glanced around the shop for any witnesses. Still the only one inside, he collected a sample of the fur and stuffed it in his pocket. He knew in his heart that Maurice was somehow involved. The raccoon's behavior was too strange, too risky for the murder to be a random coincidence. The last thing Cal needed was Woods folk prodding him about their rumored history—or worse, Winifred's whereabouts. Were there more animals infected? Had the beast that took his wife also claimed Duchess? He needed time to think, to interview Billiam alone, but with two-thirds of the Woods milling around outside, he couldn't think of a way to do so without looking suspicious. Cal balled up the handkerchief and tossed it over his shoulder, cursing himself for continuing to be a step behind.

* * *

As fast as Cal ran from the bog, he'd arrived at the bell near the General Store to find most of his neighbors had beat him to the punch. Otters, pigs, opossums, deer, badgers, rabbits, beavers, squirrels, porcupines, and more, to include an assortment of nosy birds high above in the trees. The animals stood about in animated discussion, their children close, streaked with paint, glue and bits of streamer, having come from the nearby clearing, where Cal would come to find Billiam had left them unsupervised, "working" on decorations for the Moon Festival. It appeared as if they mostly decorated each other instead.

"Dad!"

His pups shouted in unison, sprinting to Cal, throwing themselves into his arms, their combined weight knocking him backward onto his rump. They nuzzled their father, raving about the need to tell him about their day, about something that had happened to them outside of school. But it had to wait—the bell, whatever emergency had brought them together, came first.

"Boys. Boys! Calm down. All in due time, but I need to know what's going on."

"Mr. Billiam pulled on the bell," Franklin said. "We heard Ms. Duchess was *murdered*."

"We wanted to go inside to see her like all the adults, but Mr. Billiam wouldn't let us," Gus added, eyes wide with fear-tinged excitement.

Murdered? Cal stared at his children in stunned silence. How could this happen? He looked past them then, out into the surrounding darkness. Had the beast that doomed Winifred found its way into the Woods? Could this be the work of another infected? Everyone around them seemed fine, loved ones accounted for. Still, his mind raced with possibilities.

"Everyone went inside?"

"Everyone but the kids," Franklin said. "The parents took turns watching us to make sure we didn't sneak off."

Gus sniffed the night air, picking up an interesting scent. "They were wondering where you were."

The few innocent words crushed against Cal's heart and tears welled in his eyes. "I'm sorry I wasn't here sooner, boys. I came as fast as I could." He hugged them tight against himself, sniffling back tears as he struggled to hold himself together. He held them against his chest until they began to squirm, Franklin terribly embarrassed of the emotional display in front of his friends.

"Let me see you." Cal began with Franklin, patting him down, inspecting him for bite marks in the dim light of the moon. "Are you feeling okay? You'd tell me if you weren't feeling well, right?"

"Dad, *stop*. We're fine," Franklin whined, fighting his off his father's tickling paws.

Cal stood and removed a bit a streamer from behind Gus's left ear. "Come on then, let's go see our friend."

* * *

The three approached the largest of the gatherings, the group's attention focused on the badger who stood at the center of the semi-circle. Arnold, hooves on his hips, looking disgruntled as ever, saw Cal coming, and said, "Nice of you to join us. That solves one mystery."

"He looks pretty clean to me," added Meryl, the rabbit wiping at her pink, runny nose. "His coat would have been soaked." Murmurs of agreement followed around the group, though Cal couldn't tell from whom. He could barely contain his anger at the thought of being accused of such an atrocity.

"Something either of you need to get off your chest?" Cal asked, a paw on each of his pups, guiding them forward. "Have we reached a point where a mere absence is akin to guilt? I don't see your wife among us. Have her whereabouts been vetted?"

"And neither yours," Arnold snickered. "I'm just glad your boys have some supervision on a night like tonight. Who knows what's out there." Wes, Beatrix's father, thumped his beaver tail. "Can it, Arnold. We've got too much on our plate to be bickering. No one here among us murdered anyone. Let's concentrate on the facts of Billiam's story and work together so we can go home."

Upon hearing his name, Billiam turned from a side conversation, lighting up at the sight his newly arrived friend. The two formed a quick embrace, Billiam promising to tell Cal everything, but first it was necessary that Cal see the aftermath inside the general store. Billiam's account of the evening's events wasn't complete without witnessing the scene firsthand, no matter how terrible and heart-wrenching a sight. Cal left the pups with his friend, eliciting moans and complaints for not being included. He gave them each a kiss on the forehead, and promised to be right back.

* * *

Cal finished up his inspection of the tragic scene. Nothing appeared stolen, though it was difficult to tell between the chaos and otherwise barren shelves. Doubtful a simple theft-gone-wrong was the motive. Plus, Duchess had always been kind to those in need with donations and lines of credit during hard times. To have seen Duchess work so hard to carry on her mother's legacy, only to meet her end during an off week was the real tragedy. Cal returned to the group to hear Billiam explain what the others had already heard regarding his interactions with Duchess, the spoiled acorns, Sly Frances and the mud oat cakes.

"They were really quite good, but Duchess was having none of it. There must have been a fight after I left."

"So, we are in agreement that the fox is likely the one who murdered Duchess?" Arnold asked.

Billiam nodded. "I was away for only twenty, maybe thirty minutes, tops. Duchess was not happy with Frances. You all know her style of haggling—this time she went too far."

"I hear a motive," came a shout.

"She's my neighbor—my family could be in danger!"

There were screams and cries, all manner of sobbing and consoling among children and adults alike as panic spread.

Cal grabbed his friend hard by the arm, looked him in the eyes, searching for clues. The fur he'd pocketed was on the forefront of his mind. Frances's coat was a bright reddish-orange, and the evidence (evidence that he was not ready to share) suggested she wasn't present for the murder at all. "Are you certain this is the case?"

"Who else would do such a thing? Everyone seems pretty much accounted for . . ." Billiam finished at a whisper, ". . . except."

"*No.*" Cal growled through clenched teeth, squeezing hard enough to make the badger wince. They both knew Winifred was the unspoken missing animal, and that was as far as Cal would let it go.

"It's settled then," Arnold said, taking command. "I'll lead a party west toward Frances's home. With any luck, we'll quickly find the fox and return with her in custody to hear her side of the story. Wes, you're with me."

The beaver reluctantly padded over to the deer. "Last time I play cards with you."

"Who else?"

Gus latched onto his father's leg, begging for him to stay. Cal nodded, giving the pup's head a pat. The crisis had grown to involve the entire Woods. The last thing he needed to do was leave them alone, again.

Two opossums, Jarvis and Robin, chatted between themselves. They'd sent their son home with their otter neighbors for the night, and were free to volunteer. Robin raised her paw, signaling their desire to join the hunt.

Arnold ignored them, looking over the field at the many others who hid or pretended to not hear his call. When no one else spoke up or volunteered, he sighed, acknowledged the opossums at last, and waved them over. "Come on then. Try not to get yourselves eaten."

Wes pulled a small box of matches from his back pocket. He struck a match against his large buck teeth, and lit a small oil lamp. Soft glow in hand, the four set off in search of Frances.

It took the remaining Woods folk mere minutes before they grew restless and called out to Billiam, wanting to know the plan.

"What do we do now? Wait around all night?"

"What if she's out there in the dark, watching us?"

"More of us should have gone along. We need to stick together!"

Billiam anxiously tapped his paws against each other. The Woods folk were looking to him for leadership, but Cal could tell his friend was overwhelmed, unable to commit to a next step. They needed to get organized, give people jobs to keep them distracted. If the hunting party returned with Frances to find them milling about, exhausted, it would be chaos. Like tossing a hunk of cheese into the Rubbish Heap—they'd all want a piece of her.

Cal put an arm around Billiam, said, "Let's give the people something to do, shall we?" and with the snap of his fingers, began issuing orders.

"Pigs—Ted, Helen—you've got some leftover torches from your summer dinner parties, right? Let's get some light around here."

The couple thought for a moment, nodded to each other, and jogged off, arm-in-arm.

"Nutbrown." The school teacher sat with her back against a tree. She glanced up at Cal with a shocked look on her face, as if she hadn't expected to be found, or called upon. "Kids, gather 'round your teacher. She's going to tell you a story."

Nutbrown responded with a short hiss before acquiescing to the role as the kids came forward.

"Otters—Hugo, Mol—there are some extra chairs stacked in the school. Get the key from Nutbrown. We'll all help set them up."

"You got it," Mol said. He pumped a fist into the air. "Let's go, hun."

"That's the spirit," Cal said, finally feeling good about stepping up to the plate. "We can do this if we work together."

"Rabbits—Meryl, Steve—Meryl, your calligraphy is impeccable. No doubt Billiam will want a record of tonight's events. Steve, there should be paper and pencil inside the general store."

"Hold on now. Who put you in charge?" Steve, the short, stocky rabbit shot back, an arm around his wife, hugging her close. "It's true my love's handwriting is wonderful, but you seem awfully comfortable ordering us around. How do we know you aren't a suspect? Where were you this evening?"

"Out for a walk, alone." The lie spilled out of Cal before he could think otherwise. Could he let them know he'd been meeting with Maurice? What would they think? Accuse Maurice of murdering Duchess? Accuse him of being involved?

"It would seem as if you chose the wrong night to be walking around alone. Can anyone corroborate your whereabouts?" Billiam cleared his throat. "My friend is simply stepping up where I have failed. As your sole elected official, I should have the presence of mind to organize for the party's return. If they are to return soon with Frances, alive and well, a hope I dare say we all share, we must be ready."

Billiam paused, interrupted by the sound of footsteps and heavy breathing approaching from the south. GW, Hank, and Mildred entered the clearing ahead of a gaggle of boggies—turtles, frogs, newts—gasping for air.

"We ran . . . as fast . . . as we could," GW managed to get out. In a rare act, he pulled back his hoods exposing his damp skin to the cool night air.

Hank paced with his hands on top of his head, shuffling away from the group toward a clump of bushes. "Last time I drink grog . . . and go for a run."

"Please continue—we don't mean to interrupt," Mildred said.

Once they'd had a moment to compose themselves Cal took the newcomers aside, filling them in on the details as Billiam continued.

"As I was saying, we must be ready. I propose a trial. We'll question Frances and one way or another get to the bottom of the matter tonight. Our community will not sit idly by in fear when one is stolen from us in such a horrendous manner."

"And if she's guilty?" asked Hank.

Billiam shoved his paws in his pockets, sighed as he looked up, clouds blotting out much of the star-filled sky. "Then together we'll decide her fate."

* * *

The Woods folk took to their roles. At GW's direction, the bog trio paced the edge of the clearing, guarding the area, weary eyes watching for movement in the surrounding darkness. The pigs returned, loaded down with torches, a cauldron of vegetable broth, and a bushel of small bread loaves, and set up on a table Cal and Billiam hauled out from the store. They'd used the last of their flour that morning, as they had expected the general store to be restocked. While they were concerned for their ability to continue to fill their stomachs, their good nature wouldn't allow them to horde food. In such trying times, it would do the community well to spread the wealth.

Ted dug trenches in the loaves with a fork, sending Franklin and Gus away with armfuls of the soft insides to keep the children occupied while the pigs readied the impromptu meal. Licking warm soup from his paws, Cal helped hand out the steaming loaves, though he forewent one himself, his stomach anxious and unsettled. Aside from the annual Moon Festivals, there wasn't another time in recent memory when the majority of the Woods folk came together. The community was close, but there were the usual cliques, and most animals finished their days with their own kind. Despite the tragic circumstances, Cal sensed a strength in the camaraderie the murder had brought out. In a way, he'd never felt closer to his fellow neighbors. At the same time, however, part of him felt like he'd stepped back into his days with the Rubbish Heap gang, hiding what he knew might prove to be definitive evidence in the case. He put a paw into his coat pocket, felt the fur he'd taken from the scene to ensure it was still there. Protecting the community was a priority. Protecting family came first.

After the food was distributed the children broke away from Nutbrown and settled down with their parents in small clumps. Silence fell over the Woods as the animals ate, famished from work and worry. Cal took a seat on the ground next to his pups and watched them devour their supper. They both possessed a good deal of their mother's features: Gus, her cute nose and round cheeks, and Franklin, her large eyes and sharp ears. Cal had always enjoyed seeing her in them, but it didn't occur to him just how much they looked like her until now, and as he observed them, the enjoyment turned to a haunting pang of guilt, a reminder of what he'd done. A reminder not just of what he'd done, but of the secrets he held tight within, and his inability to find who'd brought the infection. Cal knew that Maurice had something to do with it. If it wasn't a member of his crew, then someone close. Why else would he be venturing so far from the Fells? Unless . . . what if a patrol had been infected, and he was out looking for the culprit too? Could they have the same goal? Above all, he needed to come clean to his pups, explain to them the circumstances and why he'd hidden the truth. But how? And when? There would never be a good time, he knew that. It was finding the right—

"Dad?" Franklin asked, mid-bite. "You're staring at us."

"Sorry, boys. I was just lost in thought."

"We skipped school and went into the Fells today," Gus blurted.

Cal started. "What?"

"Gus!" Franklin nearly fumbled the last of his meal into his lap.

"Franklin fell in a hole and an awful weasel and his rat friend tried to hurt us, but GW came and saved the day and—"

Franklin clamped a paw over his younger brother's mouth to prevent him from spilling more details. "We were supposed to ease him in—not tell Dad everything at once, you ninny."

"Wait, is this true? Franklin?" Cal felt pressure building in his skull, the kind of ache that made it feel like his head was about to pop off his shoulders. The pups looked at each other, then to their father, slowly nodding in unison. Gus began to whimper, hiding his face in his paws. Cal frowned, eyes beginning to well up at the sight.

"I'm not angry, all right? I'm just worried. You two *know* how dangerous the Fells is. How many times have I warned you?"

"A lot," Franklin muttered.

He ruffled the tops of their heads. "More than a lot. But you are okay, and that's what matters most right now."

The brothers both nodded again.

"Let's slow down and start from the beginning."

Franklin and Gus took turns adding to the story, sparing no details (and Cal suspected, embellishing a few) starting with Beatrix getting Gus in trouble and Nutbrown's reaction to Franklin sticking up for his younger brother. Cal gathered the two were proud of the moment; he had to admit, he was too. It hadn't helped that he and Billiam had riled up their teacher by distracting the students, or whatever sort of trespass she'd accused them of. After they were done Cal embraced them both—hugged them tight and thanked them for their honesty.

To think he'd let the vermin go, only to have them endanger his pups. It was a mistake he would not soon forget, nor forgive himself for in the slightest. The obvious occurred to him: that they were all in the Fells at the same time. He didn't want to press them after all they'd been through, but he couldn't help but ask one question:

"Why did you go to the Fells?"

Gus looked as if he might cry, again. His brother glared at him.

"What is it, son?"

Gus flashed a look at Franklin, then turned away, eyes on the ground. "We were—"

Franklin shushed his brother, cuffing him on the shoulder.

A short whistle sliced through the moment, snagging the attention of the three dogs; their ears perked up, turned to face the direction of the sound. Squinting, Cal could just make out a shadow of GW. The toad stood beside a thick oak in the distance, one webbed hand on his harpoon gun, the other beckoning him over.

"Stay here and don't move," Cal instructed his pups. "We'll continue this when I return." Cal jumped up and hurried over, his legs sore from sitting on the hard earth.

"What is it? Anything?"

GW shook his head. "Walk with me."

The two went west along the perimeter, away from prying eyes and ears. After a long minute, Cal could no longer stand the silence and spoke up.

"Before you start . . . the boys told me about the incident in the Fells. If you hadn't been there—"

"No thanks necessary. It's all part of the job. We're fortunate things worked out the way they did."

"Fortunate—GW, you saved my entire *world*. I can't even begin to express how on today of all days . . ." Cal trailed off, unable to find the words. "If there's anything I can ever do—"

"I appreciate it, but we have more pressing matters to attend—come." The toad lead him a short distance away, keeping his attention on the perimeter while he spoke.

"Maurice made a rare appearance at the Drinkery earlier this evening, offering to buy a round. He mentioned something about a sickness infringing on the Woods, specifically you and your family. I am hoping you weren't the source of it.

"It was obvious he was fishing for information, going about it in a rather brash way. I didn't care for his tone or the mud he slung when no one spoke up. It appeared he was singling you out to tarnish your name and spread rumors."

"Did he say anything else?"

"I didn't stick around. It upset me, and I'd had enough after the events in the Fells." GW chuckled then, adding, "though look at me now, playing sentry while Arnold is off having a go at soldier for the night."

Cal thanked him for the information, trying to process Maurice's apparent desire to blame Winifred for the infection while balancing everything else on his plate. As they continued, Cal thought he smelled a hint of the Rubbish Heap on the breeze. A sharp sour smell that made his nose tingle, his fur stand on end.

"Did you smell that?"

"What do you think I am, a dog?"

They enjoyed a good chuckle at that, the bad joke loosening the tension. Cal brought his sleeve to his nose and detected hints leftover from his engagement with Maurice. The coat was long overdue for a good wash.

"I'm sorry you have to put up with so much grief while protecting the school. I'm sure, deep down, Arnold and others acknowledge your importance. I've done a poor job sticking up for you."

"Nothing new since I returned home from the war. Boggies can be just as bad—anxious around me when the topic comes up and what they can ask. Jealous, perhaps, of my decision to go while they stayed behind. I stopped analyzing, searching for reason long ago."

"I'm sorry to hear that."

"Is what it is. I'll tell you what, though—I understand the haunting that comes with a decision to fight or stay behind, regardless of a boggie's decision. I go to sleep with it every night. You Woods folk haven't had your war, and that's a good thing, of course. But some desperately wish they had it coming. Whether that wish holds true when it's staring them in the face is a whole other story."

Cal nodded, contemplating the toad's words.

"Sometimes I feel as if my life has been a series of wars, and I had very little say in the matter."

"Then I should be the one feeling sorry for you."

They walked the remainder of the route in silence, circled a cluster of evergreens and headed back.

"One more thing before I go," Cal whispered. "Did my boys mention anything about why they went into the Fells?"

GW looked away toward the dark.

"I may have overheard some talk . . ."

A dim light appeared through the trees in the distance, northwest of their position.

"Looks like we may have some visitors." GW readied his weapon. "Look sharp."

"What did you overhear?"

"Given my place at the school I tend to overhear a lot, and I make it a priority to stay out of other's business and avoid gossip. I'm going to make an exception given the circumstances."

Cal impatiently ground his teeth. "And?"

GW studied Cal's eyes in the dim light. "Do you really not know?"

Cal shook his head no, his guts aching with anxiety over the truth he feared coming.

GW stepped close to Cal, whispering into his ear. "They were looking for their mother."

14

"Left. Left. Left, right, left," Arnold boomed from the rear as the hunting party approached the clearing. Wes led the single-file line with his oil lamp in hand, its sputtering light guiding the way. He kicked his short legs out to the rhythm, his beaver tail thwacking the ground to mark each set of steps. Behind him marched the two opossums, Robin and Jarvis, their knees pumping high into the air. Last came Arnold, dipping his head every few beats to prod a hunched-over figure forward with his great antlers. The figure continually failed to step to his beat, feet shuffling forward, defeated. The Woods folk buzzed with the party's return and quickly gathered together, forming a rough semi-circle to greet them.

"Stand back, everyone," Billiam shouted, arms out, waving his constituents back. "Remain calm and keep your children close. We don't know what we're dealing with yet."

As the party drew closer to the perimeter, it became clear that the figure being forced along was none other than Sly Frances, her wrists bound together in front with twine so thick and gnarled it resembled a tree root. She looked disheveled, bloodied and beaten, her shoulders curled forward, head down, eyes focused on the ground in front of her feet. GW visibly relaxed, lowering the harpoon gun, holding up a webbed hand to acknowledge their arrival. Arnold gave them a salute (and to Cal alone, a wink), and continued to call out marching orders as Cal and GW escorted them in. Cheers from the Woods folk in recognition of the successful hunt turned to gasps as Frances's condition was illuminated by torch light, which transformed her from shadow to a ghastly, half-dead monster.

The fox was filthy from head to toe, her fur crusted with mud and dirt. Her green turtleneck was torn and frayed and spattered with blood. Similarly, her snout, jaw, and arms up to her manacled wrists were caked in gore, enough to cause Ted to faint into the arms of his wife, and elicit cries of "Murderer!" from the crowd.

Cal looked on, stunned in disbelief. It couldn't have been Frances. He stuffed a paw in his pocket and palmed a bit of the fur he'd taken from the murder scene. Twice he glanced down at it to confirm again and again that it most certainly did not belong to the sly fox. He stuffed the evidence back in his pocket, puzzled. Compared to Frances's appearance, the four hunters appeared to have barely broken a sweat. Frances must have come along willingly, without much of a struggle, if any at all. But why?

Frances looked around at the Woods folk—most of whom she'd known for years, some her entire life—wide-eyed and bewildered as the party came to a halt. Her focus settled on Billiam, the two connecting for a moment before Arnold placed a hoof firmly on her shoulder and her gaze returned to the ground at her feet.

"Mission accomplished!" Wes boasted to more cheers, beaming with pride. "We did it!"

"Now hold on, folks." Arnold guided Frances toward the crowd to a mixture of jeers and hisses as onlookers backed into each other, stepping on hooves, paws, tails, and more to make way. He held up a hoof calling for quiet. "Before we kick off this circus, I want to fill you in on our apprehension of the suspect you see before you—provide a little context on what went down. But first, I'd like to highlight the team—including myself, of course—they're your true heroes tonight. Let's give them another round of applause."

Arnold basked in the adoration, waiting for the celebration to die down before he continued.

"Wes, that beaver can work an oil-lamp like you wouldn't believe. Now, you might think I'm being facetious, but there's not a lot of fuel in that baby, and boy did he make it count."

As if on cue, Wes's lamp went dark. Several rabbits in front gasped in amazement.

"Look at that!" Arnold clapped his hooves together, the sound like two large stones knocking against each other. "I can hardly believe it."

Wes lifted the lamp high to inspect the filament—in disbelief at the timing—to more applause.

"That brings me to my two new favorite opossums. These little guys . . . I'm not going to lie—they looked like bait to me."

Arnold paused for a laugh. The few deer who found it funny, chuckling in the back, were quickly silenced by glares.

"I know, I know, I'm being harsh. Don't worry about their feelings, I told them as much on our way out. But— *but*—listen now—let me tell you, I thought my nose was good. These two smelled the blood on our target from a quarter-mile away. Honed right in. Half bloodhound. Kept all the good genes for themselves and passed the rest to Cal. Am I right? Dogs: what are they good for when you've got opossums? And Robin here? *No fear.* Incredible. This sly fox turned to run and Robin jumped right in her path, all claws and teeth, tongue wagging, snarling. Insane. You'd have to see it to believe it. Let's give them another cheer."

The crowd erupted, the smaller species of the Woods ecstatic for the hero they'd never known living among them. Billiam stepped out of the crowd, cleared his throat loud in an effort to draw attention to himself. Cal, sensing Billiam's frustration, cut across the semi-circle. He slipped a paw under Billiam's left arm, pulling him tight against him, whispering, "Not now," through clenched teeth.

"He's making a mockery of this affair. What's next, parlor tricks? Stealing my official position out from under my nose? I'm the elected badger of the Woods folk, damn it. I have to put a stop to this."

"Let him have his moment. Save the fight for the trial, when it matters."

"Look around you, Cal. The trial has already begun."

222

Arnold waited until he once again became the focus of the crowd. "Now that we've covered the good, let's get back to that context I mentioned. After all, tonight is not a night for celebration. We've come together in a state of emergency, seeking the fugitive who so ruthlessly murdered our dear Duchess.

"When we happened upon Miss Frances, she was knee deep in her second wild turkey. Apparently, it's a weakness of their species. Isn't that right, Frances?"

"Yes." Frances sniffled, wiped a bit of mud from nose. "Yes, that is correct."

"It was explained that apparently when a hungry fox sees a wild turkey, they lose control of themselves. This goes doubly for Frances here, whose favorite food is turkey, and is likely to pounce even when she's not especially hungry, as was the case tonight."

Frances nodded, rubbing her wrists.

"Now, I'm having difficulty believing this, but I'm a big, strong deer, so what do I know? According to Miss Frances, wild turkeys can put up quite a fight, hence the mess you see before you."

Frances nodded again, then taking a sudden step forward she blurted out, "Duchess was a friend! My heart broke at the news of her murder." A portion of the crowd responded with jeers and boos that drowned out her words.

"I'm innocent!" Her voice shook as she tried to shout over the Woods folk. "Ask Billiam! Ask him if I would commit such a terrible crime."

Arnold pulled the fox back, furious with her outburst. "Did I say you could speak? How many times did we go over this?" He bent down, his face inches from Frances's own, causing her to pull away. Cal couldn't make out what followed but it was obviously some kind of threat given the way Frances cowed to his act. Had Arnold coerced her somehow into returning with them? To his memory, Frances wasn't one to back down from a fight, but the only ones who knew what happened out there were the five before him, and no one appeared to want to talk anything but turkey.

Several in the crowd had had enough, calling for her head as Arnold continued to lecture Frances. Cal thought of Billiam's account of Frances and her mud oat cakes, the scene in the aftermath, the savagery of the attack, the fur. None of it added up. The fox didn't appear to show any of the symptoms Winifred exhibited at her worst when he . . . Cal stopped himself from going further. To step up and make an argument for Frances's innocence would expose everything he'd worked so hard to hide and put his family's safety in jeopardy. He was so close to finding her killer. Between Maurice and Duchess and—

Billiam ripped his arm from Cal's grasp, stepping out from the semi-circle to confront Arnold.

"That's enough! Everyone calm down. If we're to have a trial, *as planned*, we require process, and this charade is nothing of the sort. Mol and Hugo—thank you, again—took the time to set up the chairs from the school, so let's have some order, take a seat and get this right."

Jeers and shouts continued from the raucous crowd, threatening to overwhelm Billiam's speech. The badger snarled and turned to face Arnold. With a smirk, the deer looked him in the eyes, raised his arms, hooves motioning for the Woods folk to quiet—which they did.

"Friends, neighbors . . . our sole elected official, ever the presence of reason, is right. The hour draws late. We've had our fun, and now it is time to continue with the business at hand."

"We're tired," one of the rabbits at the front complained. "Let's hang her and get this over with!" The dozen or so surrounding rabbits shouted in agreement, bouncing up and down with excitement.

"Wild turkeys don't bite! I smell a cover-up!" another said.

"And how would you know?" Billiam shot back.

"Now, now—," began Arnold, losing his grip on the crowd.

"Come on, Arnold!" yelled one of the deer toward the back. "Look at her—she's guilty!"

A group of deer chanted "Guilty," thrusting their hooves into the air. Within seconds the chant spread among the Woods folk, beating back Arnold and Billiam's attempts at regaining order.

As the justice-hungry mob closed in around Frances, the wind picked up, ruffling the torches as it swirled and changed direction. A light breeze blew across the clearing and brought with it fresh scents from the east. Billiam paused mid-sentence, his throat sore from shouting and sniffed the air. "What's this?"

Cal's mouth watered, his stomach growled. He smelled it too. Almost at once the shouts dissipated, replaced with the sound of active noses, the whole of the Woods folk sniffing the air, searching for the source of the scent that morphed between sweet and savory, piney and sour. For well over a minute, the din paused and those present sniffed at the air, as animals by nature are at their most greedy when it comes to scent—even those with a poor sense of smell, or a stuffy nose, as they only work that much harder to keep up with their neighbors. The evening was put on hold, all sense of purpose forgotten in the moment as one by one the Woods folk turned to face east to witness the missing caravan creak into view.

The Two Old Cats had arrived.

15

The Two Old Cats caravan had seen better days. From cat to moose to wagon, at a mere glance one could tell all involved were well past their prime. The covered wagon creaked and cracked and moaned as Buford, the steadfast and haggard moose, nursed it along through the sodden earth, neck yoke pressing against his fur. He grunted every other step, the strain of pulling a heavy load wearing on his mature physique. The way the wagon's four wide-spoked iron tires left deep ruts in its wake, it seemed as if the only force keeping it from getting stuck was the momentum of the moose's endless plodding steps.

Maude, one of the two ancient sisters who maintained the caravan, sat atop the front of the wagon, reins held loosely in her cream-colored paw. She wore an ill-fitting tan duster that hung loose over her frail form like a bed sheet, its bottom caked with mud. On her head, canted over one ear, was a top hat, the very top of which was sliced open like a tin can creating a flap that popped up and down with each bump like the cap of a tea kettle. Behind her, hidden within the bonnet, emanated the smells of the wagon's packed stores which had so captivated the Woods folk—and still did, as they looked on in surprise at the sight of the caravan, unsure of what to make of its appearance.

The closer Buford pulled the wagon, the more Cal was left with an unpleasant aftertaste, a sour tang on the back of his tongue. He spat a wad of saliva into the dirt, snapping out of the aftertaste's spell.

Billiam scoffed, throwing his arms up into the air. Had the badger possessed a hat, he would have thrown it to the ground and stomped it into the mud in disgust.

"Of course. *Now* they show up." He stormed over to the wagon, shaking his finger at Buford. "What do you have to say for yourself?"

The moose frowned, said in a slow drawl, "Oh, I'm just along for the ride. I let Boss do the talking." The moose's response came in such a nonchalant manner that Cal thought for a moment that Billiam might reply with a hard slap out of spite but the badger managed to channel his anger elsewhere and continued onto the driver.

"You are more than a week late. The situation has turned from bad to worse, and you've interrupted our trial to boot." Billiam stood tall, paws on his hips. "I demand an explanation! The citizens of these fine woods deserve as much, as a start."

Maude gave a weak tug on the reins with a flick of her wrists, calling Buford to a stop. She looked at Billiam, her face blank, devoid of emotion.

"Nothing?" Billiam asked. "The nerve. Do you want to know what happened here tonight? I'll tell you—our lovely Duchess was murdered behind the counter of her shop. How does that make you feel, cat?"

Maude slowly swiveled her head around, looking out over the crowd while Billiam continued to berate her.

"Bet you're in shock. You better be. If you'd been on time, all of this could have been avoided."

Billiam stepped forward and rapped his knuckles hard against the side of the wagon. "Hello? Anyone home?"

Buford cleared his throat. "She's been like this for days— ever since Lenora disappeared. We've been circling through the other territories, handing out flyers. I'm sorry we're late."

"What happened to, 'I'm just along for the ride,'" Billiam said, mimicking the moose's slow speech.

"That's true," Buford replied with a shrug, rattling the chains attached to the yoke. "I just go where I'm told."

"Well, apology not accepted. What's done is done and the best we can do is to get the wagon unloaded and you on your way before this interruption derails our entire night."

Billiam turned back to Maude, waving a paw above his head to get her attention. "Maude—yes, over here, focus on me. Now then, as you are now well aware of the fact that Duchess is no longer with us, and since she had no kin to assume control, I, Billiam Badger, sole elected official of the Woods, will take possession of the supplies and see that they are managed until we have the details sorted out. Hand me the bill of goods, madam. We'll unload them and get you on your way, post-haste."

Maude stared at the badger for a long moment, then picked up a paper from a stack beside her and held it up so Billiam and the other Woods folk could get a good look.

"Have you seen my sister?" she asked, pointing to what surely was supposed to be an illustration of her sister, Lenora. To Cal, and anyone more than ten feet away, it looked like she'd spilled ink on the page and swirled it around. "She's gone missing. It's been four days. Please, if anyone has seen her . . ."

"Don't tell me you drew that yourself. What is that, charcoal?" Billiam scoffed. "Are you blind? That looks like a raccoon."

Billiam climbed up the first rung on the side of the wagon and snatched the drawing from her paws. He jumped down waving it to the crowd.

"Anyone seen her sister? Looks nothing like this."

He took the drawing deeper into the crowd. "Anyone? No cats hiding among us?" When no one spoke up, Billiam dropped the paper in the mud at his feet, cutting his way back through the herd, clapping imaginary dust from his paws. "Come on then, no time to waste."

Urged forth by the plethora of smells, Woods folk of all kinds filed in behind Billiam, eager to assist with the unloading. He helped them organize toward the rear of the wagon, forming a line and instructing them to unload everything until Maude provided him with a bill, at which time they could perform a closer inspection. It was good enough that since Duchess's stores were nearly depleted, surely that meant most (if not all) of the wagon's contents were destined for the shelves.

Cal waited patiently for his friend to conclude business with the caravan. As the night continued, his sense of urgency rose. He needed to confide in Billiam, as least some of what he knew, but to interrupt would only worsen the badger's sour mood. Cal needed him focused and clear of distraction (as much as one could be on such a night) if he was to risk everything.

Cal looked around. The Woods folk who weren't helping unload the truck milled about, passing the time by whatever means. He walked over to his pups and guided them to a row of chairs. His feet were sore, and it felt good to take a load off. Across the aisle and closer to the front of the setup, Arnold and his team sat with Frances between them. The buzz of the celebration had faded and left them slumped and bored-looking. What a sight! Cal chuckled at the thought, even as a deep sadness returned its grip on his chest. The little bursts of light kept him going.

* * *

Maude sat hunched atop the wagon, arms folded in her lap. The wood beneath her creaked and cracked as, one by one, the animals removed the crates and packages from the back. The sensation reminded her of her youth spent working the docks, the ships rocking gently in the sea. She missed those brine-infused days. Not once did she look over her shoulder to see what the Woods folk were carrying off. It was true most of the goods were bound for the General Store (working the routes as long as she had, the orders came back to her with ease), but she no longer possessed the energy nor cared enough to inspect. Her entire world had been thrown into a tailspin since her sister's disappearance. After all, the caravan had been a means for them to travel together—less a business and more a way of life. Always on the move, nothing to hold them down. It was that sense of adventure and discovery that had kept them strong going into the twilight of their lives, careening around the bend with youthful curiosity. They'd made a pact when they were younger to squeeze every drop out of life, to make their days full of wonder—and true to form, they had.

Now, the longer Lenora was gone, the more Maude felt time creep its way into her bones. Her teeth ached, claws curled with arthritis, joints wobbly and weak, infallible memory beginning to stumble. But the most painful by far was the longing that gripped every ounce of her being. It stung like ice against her flesh, an itch she was powerless to scratch.

Maude placed a paw on the stack of flyers, tracing the outline of her sister's face. Yes, she'd drawn them herself, and yes, she knew they weren't perfect, but it was the best she could do in her state. Still, it hurt to see it reflected in the way the badger mocked her to the crowd, the way they looked at her like she was some crazy old lady who'd lost her marbles. It was the same everywhere they'd traveled during their search—the longer it went on, the greater distance folks kept, as if she were carrying some awful disease.

Maude looked up from the drawing, felt the pace of her frail heart quicken. Away from the crowd, something on the far side of the clearing lurked near a torch. She shot to her feet and grasped the cover behind her to steady herself. Her eyes flitted between the flyer and the distant shade. Had her imagination conjured another ghost to chase? Had she finally gone over the edge and tipped into madness? Onlookers and their judgment be damned—what remained of her pride was a small sacrifice to pay for a wisp of hope.

"Lenora?" she mouthed. As if sensing the attention, the figure—now definitely more real than imagined, Maude determined—slipped away from the flickering light into the shadows of nearby trees.

Moving at the speed of a nimble cat half her years, Maude hooked a paw inside the front wagon bow and swung around the side of the wagon. She landed with a foot on each side of the ladder, and slid down, hitting the ground with an "oompf" as pain shot up her legs, finding a home in her knees and hips. Something popped as she stood, which forced her to stumble forward as sharp pains threatened her momentum. Few Woods folk looked on as she recovered her balance, fighting through the discomfort to make her way across the field. When she reached the lonely torch, she began to call out for her sister—first at a whisper, then louder as she grew more confident.

"Lenora—I know you're out there! This time it's true. Why are you hiding? Come back to me."

Maude circled farther from the safety of the torch light, paws out in front, testing the thick darkness. When she received no response, she returned to the torch. She gripped its base with both paws, twisted her hips and pulled, ripping it from the ground.

"It's me, Maude—your sister!" The old cat swung the torch out in front of her in a wide arc, beating back shadows as she changed direction, cutting to her right. "I've been looking everywhere for you. Please come home," Maude begged as her courage began to falter, hope wavering like it had each of the past several nights. She reminded herself to stay strong with a quick pep talk. "We promised each other we'd never leave this world alone."

As Maude turned away, a figure to her left stirred, just out of view. Lenora rose to her feet like a nightmarish revenant wrapped in the blanket she'd stolen from the general store. She took a step forward, then another, and another, then, SNAP—her foot landed on dry twig.

"Lenora?" Maude spun, torch held aloft.

Maude barely had time to gasp before Lenora struck, hissing as she leapt at her sister. Lenora raked her face, claws ripping through fur, eye, and nose, then bit down on her collar bone. Maude screamed, dropping the torch as she fell backwards, flailing to protect herself, beating at her attacker.

Flames spilled from the torch as it fell to the ground and bounced against a trailing corner of Lenora's blanket, igniting it in a flash. Fire shot across the blanket and engulfed Lenora's back. Lenora threw herself from her downed sister. The blanket clung to her as she thrashed about. She screamed in horror, unable to shake the blanket free while she wildly whirled across the field toward the caravan.

The scene turned to chaos and confusion as the Woods folk scattered en masse and fled from the burning figure charging in their direction. Billiam shouted for calm, unsure of the cause for panic. Cal grabbed his pups, one under each arm, and ran toward the General Store to escape the mob as a group of terrified deer, ignoring commands from Arnold, trampled their way through frightened rabbits, opossums, and others. GW ran toward the threat, flashbacks of the war hitting him at full speed. He dropped to a knee and took aim, but a clear shot was impossible to find as hysterical Woods folk passed between him and Lenora, unaware of his attempt to end the situation.

Buford bellowed in fright, his deep voice driving the nearby animals away in a panic as they distanced themselves from the muscled beast. He dug his hooves into the earth, attempting to pull the wagon with all his might, but the brake block had been placed beneath one of the rear wheels and the wagon refused to move. Arnold stepped forward, locking antlers with Buford, and demanded that he remain calm and control himself.

Lenora whirled past Buford and slammed into the side of the wagon. The impact finally ripped the searing blanket from her back, taking strips of charred and smoking fur with it. Around the caravan, the last of the Woods folk unloading goods dropped their cargo where they stood and fled.

Arnold took a step back, wide-eyed at the carnage. Buford craned his head to see flames spread out across the bonnet, licking their way toward his carriage, and, spooked, all instinct gave way to panic. He threw his head forward, locked back up with Arnold, then turned and whipped his neck to the side, tossing the deer away like he was nothing. Buford lurched forward once more, his hooves repeatedly sliding through muck, until one of his rear legs stumbled onto a large rock. He surged ahead, every last ounce of strength devoted to tearing himself free. The block cracked under the extreme pressure and splintered apart and to set the wheels in motion. Buford briefly stumbled, and then, upon recognizing his sudden freedom, galloped forward, the burning wagon careening behind him. Woods folk fled being trampled as the moose changed directions at random, unable to shake the growing fire.

Buford careened into the trial setup, sending chairs flying into the air, shattering one of the tables and destroying the arrangement Billiam had worked so hard to pull off. Frances did not want to exacerbate a terrifying situation, and so remained seated for the impending trial, even after her guards fled their positions. But with Buford charging for her, Frances ran from her designated holding area. Six steps from her chair her foot caught a divot and she tumbled out of harm's way as the Moose charged past.

Hank tucked his head and limbs against his shell as the wagon fish-tailed out, knocking him away. Mildred screamed for her fallen friend, running from the relative safety of the caravan's wake to his aid. Buford cut a tight turn at the sound of the salamander's voice, galloping in her direction, the wagon briefly up on two wheels, threatening to roll, before crashing back down, bouncing on all four. GW saw the coming interception and chanced a shot.

The bolt flew, striking the wagon between two spokes of the left rear wheel, punching deep into the crackling wood. As the wheel continued to turn, the iron spokes struck the shaft, sending it wobbling off kilter, ripping it from the fire-weakened axle, spinning underneath the carriage. Somehow the wagon managed to remain upright, allowing the moose to continue his charge. GW threw down his weapon, sprinting across the field waving his arms, screaming for Mildred's attention as Buford bore down on her. When she finally saw him, she glimpsed back over her shoulder to see the moose right behind her. Wide-eyed with terror, she pumped her arms, changing directions—cutting left, then right—but still the moose gained. GW launched himself into the air, arms outstretched to knock Mildred out of the way. They locked eyes seconds too late, inches too far, as Buford ran her down, hooves stamping her into the earth. GW's momentum continued and he crashed against the spokes of the front wagon wheel, and was knocked back, beaten and bruised. The rear of the wagon continued over his prone form, the wheel severing his left arm at the elbow joint through both winter layers and bone. Buford cut another sharp turn. The front axle cracked and the wagon rocked to the side. The snap echoed across the clearing as the wagon broke from the tongue that connected it to the yoke around the moose. The flaming wreck rolled over and over, three times before coming to a rest on its side. Buford let out a hoarse cry and continued north. He fled the scene, desperate, as the fire continued up the tongue toward the yoke, spurring him on until he disappeared, eaten up by the dark.

16

The old cat fled north from the chaos, pushing aside the throbbing pain of her old, aching muscles, the sickening scent of her own toasted fur and scorched flesh compel ing her on, running through the Woods toward the Fells. Two personas dueled within her, sparring for attention and acceptance in the background as the infection took full control of her body. Lenora, Clem— whomever she was—was of no concern compared to the matter of her survival. Only instinct remained.

She remembered little since sundown aside from the sting of burns and the roar of fire pushing back against her seemingly insatiable madness, filling her with nausea and guilt. She should never have left the safety of the underground chamber. Maurice had fed her and provided a warm, dry place to stay. She'd been a fool to take such a gift for granted after being lost for so long. The raccoon had been the only one to care for her, to show appreciation for her, and then the sickness running rampant in her veins had to go and destroy everything. She was aware of it now, at least in the moment as her body operated without her input and pushed itself to the brink, frothy spittle dripping from her bloody lips. Perhaps, if she could only slip back inside undetected, she could act as if she'd been there all along, go back to the way things were. She realized now that more than anything she wanted to be home—a place where she could curl up and drift off into nothing. The Rubbish Heap might be the only place left to take her in, willingly or otherwise.

17

The scene in front of the General Store was full of scattered bodies, chewed up earth, and sputtering flames. The injured bleated like dying sheep, crying out for help, in shock. Cal secured Franklin and Gus with a group of children under the care of Helen, who'd single-handedly managed to drag her husband and son to safety by their corkscrew pig-tails after they'd fainted at first sight of the attacker—a screeching *thing* flailing its limbs while wrapped in a blanket, *on fire*—a blazing mini-tornado headed right for them. Everyone in the vicinity was shaken by the events, including the pups, who clung to each other, shivering. Cal removed his coat and draped it over their shoulders, then pulled them into a strong hug. He promised he'd be right back, lying that he needed to check on others, help with the wounded. It pained him to continue to withhold the truth, but he didn't have time to explain his actions. The question of the identity of the attacker nagged him. He kicked at a cluster of acorns, sending the half-eaten bunch into the shadows. Cal followed it along and kicked the farthest flung acorn again and again as he processed the chaos. He thought back to the "missing" poster—Maude's poorly drawn cat in stripes of gray and black. As he played with the bits of fur in his pocket, it struck him—the coats were certain to be a match. Lenora was to blame for his wife's death. The more he walked, and the more he mulled the facts, the more he was sure of it. The cat's long absence was explainable by the infection, and for why she would have been covered with mud and debris, unrecognizable to Winifred at a glance after being bitten. The smell of charred decay as she'd whirled about the clearing—it had been her hiding in the dark on the perimeter all along, remaining close to the murder scene after ambushing Duchess. The signs of sickness were clear—the docile old cat replaced with a monster. He should have trusted his instincts, pushed GW to search the area with him. If Arnold and his crew hadn't arrived with their prisoner . . . Cal didn't have to time to mull hypotheticals. There wasn't a moment to lose. The cat had run north, but there was no guarantee she'd return to the Fells. Her scent wouldn't linger forever and the longer he waited, the harder she would be to track.

The wagon still burned on the far side of the clearing. The bonnet was long gone, leaving the series of smoldering bows exposed like ribs, the last of the caravan's goods spilling out between them. The image gave Cal pause—he was overcome with a flashback to the burning schoolhouse—the burns across his back, bursting out the window, kids tucked against him. He looked away, back at his pups one last time—still huddled together under his coat, engaged with the other children around them—and promised himself he'd explain everything when this was done.

Billiam stood in the heart of it all, pointing, shouting for folks' attention as animals ran past him with little acknowledgment, rounding up their loved ones and scurrying off in search of home. Any moment now, out of exasperation he'd collapse to the ground in a heap. All he wanted to do was help—why wouldn't anyone listen? He caught sight of Cal out of the corner of his eye (after a quick double-take, having seen the dog in only an old white t-shirt, absent his coat) and called out, opting to chase after him when he didn't respond.

"I'm talking to you, buddy," he said, grabbing his friend's shoulder.

"I need to go," said Cal, shrugging him off.

"What do you mean you need to go? Look at this place! This is a disaster. A week spent wandering the countryside for her sister, and here of all places. Remind me next time a family member goes missing to just let them go. I don't have the stomach for this stuff."

Cal continued, ignoring his friend. Billiam jogged out in front of him, stretched himself wide, arms out to block the way.

"We need you here, Cal. There'll be a time for vengeance on behalf of our community, but we all sensed it in the store—a blight is upon us and we don't know what we're dealing with. We'll get the entire Woods working together, even Old Brown, and leave no stone unturned. Let her go."

"I can't."

"Think of your kids, Cal. Think of—"

Billiam gasped as the pieces fit together, the tragic picture a punch in his gut. "Winifred."

* * *

GW sat in the dirt next to Mildred's crumpled form, issuing orders to Hank, who'd hurried to his side in the wake of Buford's rampage. A cold sweat broke out across his entire body, soaking through his base layers in response to the severe wound, which still threatened his consciousness with each passing second, dark spots swimming throughout his vision, impossible to blink away. Following the horror of the injury, his training had kicked in and he'd focused on his breathing, willing himself to stay awake. Now the toad veteran focused on Hank, instructing him to strip the layers from the nearby severed arm—which, to GW's surprise, he did without question or disgust—discarding the winter coat sleeve in favor of the thin raincoat material beneath. Hank tied the sleeve around what was left of GW's arm, high above the stump near the armpit. With his good hand, GW pulled a spare harpoon from his quiver and, with help from Hank, slotted it through the band to form a tourniquet, twisting it around and around until the knotted rain coat threatened to pop and blood ceased to trickle from the wound. GW tucked the shaft of the harpoon under his arm to prevent it from slipping out, and despite pleas to take it easy, stood without assistance. He swayed as he looked down at Mildred, adjusting his feet to help his balance. Again, Hank offered aid, but GW shook him off.

"I'm fine," he said, knowing he was anything but fine. As if to underscore the point, he plucked his severed arm from the ground and slipped it—severed end first—into his quiver with the remainder of his harpoons. Hank gave him a look. GW shrugged. It didn't make any sense, but it felt right in a moment when nothing felt good. Shame wracked his psyche, hurting him more than any physical ailment possibly could. He'd failed and paid dearly for it, his friend lying dead before him, half buried from the force of the moose's hooves, looking as if she was attempting to crawl her way out of a grave. Hank bent to check on her, but GW pulled him back. He knew better—too many had fallen around him during the war for him to check himself.

"Don't."

"Don't what?"

"She's gone, Hank. You don't need the image of what she looks like under there to follow you home. Trust me."

* * *

Arnold dusted himself off, wincing as he dabbed a trickle of blood from his forehead with a hoof. That was . . . unexpected, to say the least. He'd gone unchallenged as the alpha deer for so long, it hadn't dawned on him that the moose could possibly out-muscle him. He reminded himself that a cornered animal was an unpredictable creature, capable of extreme feats, and that he shouldn't take it too hard. He briefly wondered how strong he'd be if their places were reversed, deciding Buford's sudden burst was nothing compared to what he was capable of. Nonetheless, he needed to bulk up come spring. He'd been fooled once, and there wouldn't be a second.

The deer looked around for his crew. "Wes! Robin! Jarvis! Hunting Party, form up on me! I'll be damned if we let this beast get away."

"Count me in." Frances appeared at his side, wrists still bound in twine.

"You've got to be kidding me."

"A chance to avenge Duchess's murder and assert my innocence? Whatever we just witnessed tear apart the old cat before causing all this, must have killed our dearest hedgehog, no? How can we let it get away? Speaking of which," she gestured to her bindings, "I'd appreciate if you could do me the honor. I'll need more than my wits about me."

Arnold glanced around to see who might be watching, then lifted Frances's arms up to his mouth and bit down, grinding his teeth a hair's breadth from her fur until they'd loosened enough for her to tear free from captivity.

"Easy, killer." Frances massaged her wrists—bruised, but nothing that wouldn't heal in a day or two.

"I always knew you were innocent."

"Sure sounded like it."

"Now, Frances—"

"Don't you *Now, Frances* me." The fox continued to give Arnold an earful, but the deer was no longer listening, distracted by a sudden uproar between Billiam and Cal, the badger in the dog's face, waving his arms and shouting in an awful, hoarse voice. Arnold put an arm around Frances and turned her toward the action, the pair listening in.

* * *

"Damn you, Cal." Billiam gave him a weak punch in the chest. "How could you keep such a thing from me?" He gestured to the woods folk around them, "From us?"

"Keep your voice down," Cal growled through clenched teeth. "This is not the time or place for this discussion."

"Oh, I'm sorry—and when would be a good time? Tomorrow, when a pack of squirrels shows up at my front door, foaming at the mouth? I visited your house, Cal. The missus and little ones are home right now, *supposedly* safe. We're practically neighbors, for dirt's sake. You don't think I could have used this bit of info?"

Cal glanced to the side—the Woods folk around them were beginning to take notice—coming closer, curiosity getting the best of them.

"I told you, *not now*."

"What about Duchess?"

Cal snapped, grabbed the badger by his coat and stepped forward and pulled him in, slamming their foreheads together. "How dare you put her murder on me. It was Maude's missing sister, Lenora, who committed these unspeakable acts. She'd been out there waiting, watching us since she murdered Duchess and you rang that damn bell."

"She ambushed Duchess *and* her own sister? How do you know that?" Billiam shot back, matching Cal's intensity. "How do you know it wasn't your wife?"

Cal patted his sides, realizing he'd left the fur he'd taken from the murder scene in his coat pocket. "I found bits of fur near Duchess's body. I'm certain it belonged to the killer, and that when we confront Lenora it will match."

"You hid evidence from me? Evidence that could have eliminated Frances as a suspect?"

"I planned to investigate on my own—find the killer myself. There was too much at stake."

"Because your wife is sick and you know what that means for your family."

"My wife is not sick!"

"And how do you know that? How can I trust you?"

"Because she's dead, damn it!" For the first time, Cal felt the absolute certainty of Winifred's death, that she was gone, buried, and never coming back. They'd had their last nuzzles, spent their last moments as a family, and now only emptiness remained. He loosened his grip on his friend as tears began to well. "Happy now?"

Billiam stumbled back in shock as gasps fluttered about the gathered crowd.

"Is it true, Dad?"

Cal spun at the sound of Franklin's voice. He and Gus stood at the edge of the gathering, still huddled together under Cal's coat. When Cal didn't answer, they both began to cry, fleeing the circle, leaving the coat behind.

Cal stumbled after them, falling to his knees. "Boys, wait—"

The night quieted for a long minute that felt as if it stretched on for hours. "I-I'm sorry, Cal," Billiam stuttered. "I didn't know. I didn't—"

"No, you didn't. And this"—he said, referencing his pups—"is why. Yes . . . she *was* sick . . . But you don't know what it's like to watch the one you love deteriorate before you. To have her disappear to spend the final moments of her life alone, so your last memories of her aren't of the sickness. To track her down and upend that effort, so you become the one to take her from this world, to prevent others from seeing her like that. And so you spend every waking moment hating yourself, lying to your children, unable to share the truth with anyone, until it all blows up in your face. And now the only thing you can do is return to the Fells one more time to stop Lenora, and stop the disease from spreading."

Cal pushed himself up and dusted off his paws. "So, that's what I'm going to do, if you'll kindly get out of my way."

Cal stepped past Billiam into the arms of Frances, tears streaming down her face. "I can't let you do this alone, Cal." She stepped back, leaving maroon smudges on Cal's white shirt. She chuckled through tears at the absurdity, apologized for being a mess. She licked a paw to try and wipe them off, but he stopped her, told her not to worry about it.

249

"Count me in as well," GW said, stepping forward. "No good can come from venturing north alone at this hour."

Hank cut into the loose circle, interrupting his friend. "You've got an arm off, toad. What are you going to do, sear the stump on the burning wagon?"

GW fumed, one brow raised. "What are you, mad? Get a kit from the store and we'll stitch it up right quick. I didn't save those pups to let their father sacrifice himself on my watch."

Arnold cleared his throat to draw attention to himself. "Excuse me—every team needs a leader." Frances shot him a look that read *How dare you*, in the best light. "Or, someone to guard the back."

Cal nodded, acknowledging the volunteers. "This is not going to be fun. We'll meet by the wagon in five. I need a few minutes."

Helen met Cal outside the circle, guiding him to the side of the General Store where she'd seen his pups flee. Cal found them around the back, sitting against the building, huddled together, whimpering, their eyes red from tears. When they saw their father, Franklin helped Gus to his feet, and they ran to him, throwing themselves around his waist, hugging him as if it were their last moment together, and they'd never let go. Cal hunched over and clutched them against himself, uttering not a word. There was nothing he could say. He had to go, to leave them behind once more, but he did not want to stray from their warmth. He would do so eventually, and he would leave them as much, but not now. Not yet.

PART 3

THE PIPER
AT THE
GATES OF
NIGHT;
OR, INTO
THE
UNKNOWN

18

There was no celebratory send off when the ragged crew plucked their torches and headed north. Those left behind to tend to the dead and wounded were split on if they should have departed at all. Those against argued they'd simply been unlucky, and nothing good comes from looking for trouble. Best to tend to their own and hope the infected moved on, or perished before they could harm another. The remainder felt the opposite—better to take care of the problem now than to risk foisting it on someone else. Regardless, what little, if any, sway the community held over those in the party's actions in the past was of no concern now. Decisions had been made and there was no turning back.

Cal led the way, brushing off the chill cutting through his t-shirt, his nose tracking the faint smell of rubbish that thankfully had yet to dissipate. Frances followed, torch in one paw, a claw hammer she'd "borrowed" from the General Store in the other. GW and Hank came as a pair, the tortoise refusing to leave the injured toad's side. GW swore he could operate the harpoon gun with one arm, but Hank dismissed each and every argument. "In the heat of battle, you're going to need a mate," he'd said. GW reluctantly agreed, and that was that. Hank clutched a spare harpoon, which he occasionally swung and stabbed at the night air, getting a feel for its weight (or so he claimed when GW told him to cool it and save his energy). Arnold, true to his word, brought up the rear of the pack with the beaver's oil lamp refueled and burning bright.

The journey was quiet and uneventful until they neared the river, when Arnold hissed for them to stop and take cover. He dimmed the oil lamp while Frances dropped to the ground with her torch. Hidden behind an assortment of trees, bushes and other makeshift camouflage, the five waited and listened to the sound of labored breathing closing on their position from behind. As the figure passed between them, Arnold stuck out a hoof, tripping the animal to the ground. He jumped up along with the others, flaring the lamp to full, illuminating the fallen character.

"Billiam?" Arnold asked, dismayed by the sight of the badger in his wrinkled suit coat.

The badger lay on the ground, one arm up, shielding his eyes from the light. "Looks like the coast is clear from down here. No sign of her."

Cal extended a paw, pulling Billiam to his feet. "What are you doing?"

"The more the merrier, right?"

When none were quick to agree, he added, "No one was listening to me anyway. I tried to organize the wounded, send for a doctor, check to make sure those in their homes were safe. All practical ideas to my mind."

"Sounds like your days are numbered, Mr. Sole Elected Official," Arnold said. "Another vote will be here before you know it."

"And not a moment too soon. The future fills my stomach with dread—I'm beginning to believe I'm not cut out for politics."

"Took you long enough."

"All right, enough, you two." GW hocked a thick wad of phlegm in the dirt. "We don't have time for petty squabbles."

Cal nodded. Sniffing the air, he regained the scent and motioned for the group to follow. Billiam fell in behind Cal, keeping his distance from Arnold. After crossing the river over the fallen tree, it dawned on the badger that he'd come along empty-handed. He asked Hank and GW if he could have one of *those* (a harpoon) to which he received a stern, non-negotiable, *no*. Instead of focusing on their surroundings and the whereabouts of Lenora, Billiam spent most of his time in the Fells with his eyes on the ground, looking for the right log or stick that could fend off attackers. Successful on his fifth attempt (the others too brittle, filled with rot), he carried under his arm a section of fallen tree limb so thick it took both paws to swing.

The deeper into the Fells the party went, the closer together they huddled, watching for any sign of movement. Lenora's scent danced with the foul odor of the Rubbish Heap until Cal laid eyes on the flickering torches in the distance, and the two became impossible to separate, the rubbish overwhelming all other smells. When they reached the treeline at the edge of the large clearing, Cal motioned for them to get down.

"So, this is the Rubbish Heap," Billiam whispered. Frances shushed him. "Bigger than I imagined," he continued, eliciting a follow-up flick of his ear from the fox.

Cal asked them to wait and crept forward for a better look. The torches in front of the main entrance illuminated a cluster of bodies splayed about in the dirt. Maurice lay slumped against the side of the entrance, motionless. The sight of his former friend shook Cal, and it took a moment to collect himself before returning to the group to relay the information.

"Bodies?" Billiam asked, interrupting Cal as he explained the scene in front of the Rubbish Heap. "Dead bodies—carcasses you mean. A dozen? How many are we talking?"

"Keep your voice down, Billiam," Cal said.

"What are we getting ourselves into?"

"You know exactly what we're getting ourselves into," GW whispered. "You ran after us to help, not hinder our operation. If you're not feeling up to it, turn back now before you get in the way and someone gets hurt."

Billiam, taken aback by the stern warning and focus on himself, cleared his throat and deeply exhaled. "I-I'm ready. Nothing to worry about."

Cal gave GW a nod of thanks. He put an arm around Billiam and gave his shoulder a squeeze.

"Now then, the evidence ahead points to Lenora being inside the Rubbish Heap. It's going to be tight. It's going to be dark; but the only way to be sure is to go in after her.

"Arnold—you're not going to fit. We need you to guard the entrance—keep it open for our return."

"Fine by me."

"The rest of you follow my lead and let's try not to get lost."

They ran from the treeline to the Rubbish Heap. The party, aside from Cal, slowed in shock and disbelief when they reached the bodies. GW whistled and held up his stump—a sign for the others to hold position—as he scanned the scene for threats. Over a dozen vermin lay dead—clawed, slashed, bitten, ripped apart between them and Maurice. Billiam tip-toed around the massacre as best he could, whispering, "I'm a big brave badger. I'm a big brave badger," with each step.

Hank cursed himself for coming along. "The cat did all this? And we're going in there after her?"

"Can it, Hank," GW grumbled.

"Hard to tell," Cal said. "Don't touch anything—the infection spreads through bite. Assume their blood is tainted with disease."

"Stick close, brother," GW tapped his gun lightly against Hank's shell. "We're in this together."

"Awful sight." Hank shook his head as he looked over Maurice. "Friend makes it all the way down to the bog and back for a drink, only to meet his end. What if we'd taken him up on the drink? Entertained whatever game he'd been playing for even a minute?"

"Does us no favor to fixate on what-ifs," GW said. "Maurice was up to no good in the pub. Whatever he'd been after caught up with him in the end, that's for sure."

Billiam gasped. "GW!"

"What? Were you there? He had it coming."

"Speaking ill of the dead at a time like this." Billiam dropped his log, spat on his claws, rubbing the spittle between them, up along his arms, then turned around in place two times.

GW shrugged. "What are you doing?"

"Countering your bad luck."

Cal ignored their banter and entered the mouth of the Rubbish Heap alone, his paws around his eyes to shield them from the light. After a moment he returned, asked Frances to give Arnold her torch. "One lick of flame and the entire heap could go up."

"How will we see?" Hank asked.

"Our eyes will adjust once we're inside"

"Not all of us see as well as you."

"Take the oil lamp," said Arnold, handing the light off to Frances. "There's more than enough light for me out here."

Cal eyed the lamp with grave concern. Fire was fire; no matter the form it was never allowed within the heap. But Hank was right, and they could use all the help they could get. Better to risk chance of a fire, than suffer a blind ambush.

Arnold basked in the warmth and (relative) security of the torches. The others continued, picking their way over and around the bodies. Cal paused and placed a paw on Maurice's shoulder as he picked up the raccoon's time-worn blade, taking a moment filled with mixed emotions. What Maurice had said about taking Cal in as a young pup was true, and despite the distance between them on many levels, Cal would always be indebted to him for those early days. As Cal pushed off, Maurice sputtered to life, coughing up blood. Cal and the others jumped back in surprise, weapons up, claws out.

Maurice groaned, "I'm still alive? I must have passed out." He looked down, examining himself, grimacing as he pawed at his gore-soaked mid-section. "My guts are on fire. Why did you wake me? Should have let me die in peace."

"I—," Cal stumbled in the moment.

Maurice glanced at each of the faces before him, then down at the dead crew around their feet. "At least these traitors stayed put. Clem must have finished them off and gone inside."

"Clem?" Cal asked.

"My cousin. She was long lost, but I discovered her in the Fells just yesterday, delirious with fever. Be careful, she's sick. I should have done something about it, but I was too soft—too hopeful she might get better."

Billiam pulled a crumpled note from the inside breast pocket of his jacket. He crouched down in front of Maurice, unfolding the dirt-stained paper to reveal Maude's sketch that he'd previously cast aside.

"That's her all right. She escaped while I was away. Half the heap is infected. The other half scared shitless. Hard to tell which is which, the indiscriminate backstabbers." Maurice chuckled at his own comment, laugh turning to a harsh, painful cough, spraying a bloody mist across the flyer. "If Clem hadn't shown up when she did to pull them off me, I'd be rat food by now. Probably still will be, but at least I won't be alive for the meal."

Billiam brought the flyer closer to Maurice. "Hate to break it to you, but that cousin of yours is an old cat. She's been missing for a week."

"No . . ." Maurice sighed, smacking the back of his head against the heap. "I should have known better. There were signs—she was such a picky eater. It gets so lonely out here . . . I haven't seen another raccoon in years."

Maurice closed his eyes, dead by all appearance aside from the whisper of each shallow breath. When he opened his eyes, he focused on his old friend.

"Well, I guess this is it, Cal. We—"

Cal lashed out with the blade, punching it deep into Maurice's chest, silencing the raccoon before he could utter another word. A look of shock on Maurice's face turned to a wry smile as their history died along with him.

"Better to finish him off than to let the fool suffer," GW said, breaking the silence that had fallen over the group.

Cal set a foot against Maurice's body for leverage and tore the blade free.

"Let's go."

* * *

Cal led the group further into the Rubbish Heap, Billiam at his heels (anxious and empty-handed, having grown tired of lugging his log around), followed by GW and Hank. Frances brought up the rear, light from the oil lamp illuminating the tight tunnel. So much had changed since Cal had last set foot inside the mound. It had grown exponentially in ten years, small tunnels crisscrossing through larger tunnels, leading up, down, and every which way. As they journeyed on, Cal realized he had no idea where he was leading them, or where he planned to go. He heard vermin skitter about their hidden pathways, catching a whiff of the invaders as they passed. They needed to find an access point that led downward, deeper into the heap. Cal recalled Maurice spending most of his time within the heap lurking around the lower levels of the structure. If Maurice had brought Lenora inside with the intent of keeping her away from his crew, he would have kept her close to his own quarters. Even the most bull-headed vermin stayed away from the boss's lair.

The entry tunnel dumped into a large great room complete with four petrified columns holding up the ceiling. At three times Cal's height, the room was immense, lined with more tunnels than Cal could count. Moonlight filtered in through a small hole in the center of the ceiling, highlighting a similarly sized wooden grate in the floor. The group fanned out as Cal cautiously approached the grate.

"I don't like this," GW said, backing into one of the columns, head swiveling, too many entry/exit points to effectively cover. Sounds of the heap permeated every inch of the room—scratching, scuttling, sniffing, squeaking—rebounding off walls, impossible to pin down.

Hank shivered. "You can say that again."

"I don't like this," Billiam echoed, shrugging off the hard looks as if to say, you asked for it.

Cal crouched down next to the grate, beckoning for Frances to bring the light.

"Are you sure about this?" Frances asked. "There are a lot of ways out of this room—all of them wide open except for this one."

"I'm hoping this is a shortcut." Cal squatted low, stashed his weapon at his feet and slipped his paws around the side of the grate, straining to lift the heavy cover. "Billiam—give me a hand—hurry."

The badger stepped up, putting his back into it, and together on three they lifted the grate as the floor began to rumble.

* * *

Outside, Arnold sensed the rat coming. It spun as it screamed, launching off the top of the Rubbish Heap in a daring leap that was destined to fall short. Still, Arnold stepped up, swinging the torch like a bat and belting the rat across the field into the trees. It was the third piece of filth that failed to surprise him since he'd taken post outside. As the vermin trickled back to defend their home, his confidence grew with each foiled attack, but he couldn't help feeling on edge. Fear tickled his senses—something in the way the last of the leaves flitted restlessly in the breeze, the sliver of moonlight peeking through above. Arnold stomped about the torches, fuming. So what if he was alone? He was the alpha! He rubbed a hoof along a stretch of his antlers, reminding himself of how great a specimen he'd become. These little wretches had nothing on him.

Not a half-second after the thought crossed his mind, he felt a sharp pain slice across his right calf. Arnold cried out, lifting his leg in time to avoid another swipe from a shifty weasel brandishing a jagged knife. The weasel bared its teeth, hissing. Arnold responded by stomping down, shattering the weasel's shoulder and pinning it to the ground. He stomped down again, crushing the weasel's ribcage, silencing its scream, then kicked out at another ugly vermin charging between the torches to avenge its friend. Arnold's hoof caught the scruffy thing beneath the chin, nearly taking its head clean off.

The sound of the breeze intensified as Arnold waved his torch close to the ground, warding off any more souls crazy enough to sneak up on him. It wasn't until he brought the torch back up that he realized the wind wasn't blowing—the sound was not of dry leaves, but of a tide of vermin returning to the Rubbish Heap, swarming out from the treeline, heading right for him.

Arnold hurried to the entrance and ducked down, shouting into the Rubbish Heap, his voice echoing deep within the tunnels ahead.

"Cal! If you can hear me, run! They're coming!" He dropped his torch and bolted from the clearing, pumping his arms and legs as fast as he could manage, sprinting for the safety of the river.

* * *

"That sounds like Arnold." Frances cocked her head, focused on isolating the sound.

"Do you think there's trouble?" Billiam managed through the pain of lifting the grate.

"Focus, Billiam!" Cal's legs shook as he strained to lift their side more than a few inches. Another deep breath and they had it. "Now, to the left. Frances, bring the light." Cal and Billiam managed two steps to the side before the cover slipped from their paws. It wasn't much but they'd exposed a large enough gap to fit through one at a time.

"You all felt that, right?" Billiam asked, teeth chattering as the rumble reverberated across the floor. "That can't be good."

Frances approached the gap, hovering over it with the lamp. "Nope."

A subtle movement, a twitch of a limb, caught GW's eye, but it was too late. An obese rat flopped out from a tunnel dug high into the wall, plunging down onto GW, knocking him back from the column, his gun to the side as he fired. The harpoon sailed wide, punching through two rats who raced toward the great room through yet another tunnel, pinning them to the wall. Hank was quick to respond, bashing the fat rat over the head with his harpoon. He then lowered it like a lance and charged the dazed fiend, piercing his gut, running him through.

In the center of the room, a crush of frightened, hungry vermin burst from below, swarming over Frances as she stepped back to protect herself. Frances thrashed about, smashing the lamp against the ground as she fell backwards, overwhelmed by the vicious tide. Liquid flame exploded from the fractured glass, showering the room and vermin alike, scattering the vermin away from the fox as she rolled free.

Cal picked up his blade and swung it back and forth, slicing his way through the torrent to Frances's aid. Frances brought the claw hammer down again and again as she struggled to fend off the swarm. The pair fought back-to-back, covered in a filth that made the fox's encounter with the wild turkeys a distant memory.

GW slammed his gun down, grabbed one of the harpoons that had fallen free during the skirmish, and slotted it. He picked up the gun and yelled for Hank, who turned and gave the loaded mechanism a quick pull, ratcheting the bolt home. GW bent backward and turned the weapon on Hank, his aim tracking upward. He smashed the trigger, targeting a fraction above Hank's bald head. The bolt punched through a weasel who'd managed to climb up the tortoise's back. The impact took the weasel into the air and pinned its body against the ceiling.

Hank flipped onto his back, spinning on his shell, crushing several vermin that followed in the weasel's path.

Flames quickly spread along the walls of the room, out and along several of the tunnels, cutting off the way back to the entrance. The mob arrived from outside, unable to stop their momentum as the front ranks were propelled screaming through the fire.

Billiam ran in circles, screaming at the top of his lungs in blind panic, "I'M A BIG, BRAVE BADGER! I'M A BIG

BRAVE BADGER!" He waved his arms around wildly, his long claws somehow piercing all comers like skewers through meat, forming an assortment of kebabs.

Confronted amid the chaos by the largest weasel he'd ever seen, GW reached for another harpoon, but came up short with his severed arm. The weasel cocked its head, puzzled at the sight. GW seized the opening and slapped the weasel across its face with the webbed hand. He then leapt at the dazed beast and stabbed the limb into its open maw, forcing it backward. The Most Regal Toad followed through, landing on the weasel's chest as it tripped and fell, choking the bastard with his dead limb, forcing the arm down its throat past the wrist.

Cal coughed, hunkered down searching for air. The walls had gone up, and now the fire threatened to consume the remainder of the room. The only way out was down, and he hoped there was another set of tunnels that would lead them outside. He and Frances called out to the others through the smoke, rallying the team to the center.

Cal crouched down beside the grate, preparing to descend, when Lenora slithered out from the gap in the floor, covered with gore. Cal stumbled back, the blade slipping from his grasp. Lenora looked around at the fire consuming the Rubbish Heap and screamed.

"How dare you take my home!"

She leapt through the smoke, claws out for Cal.

A deafening roar overtook the room as a massive paw swept through the ceiling intercepting Lenora mid-air and smashing her through one of the support columns and into the wall beyond, fracturing her skull and pulping her insides.

Frances grabbed Cal by the shirt-collar and yanked him away from trash collapsing overhead. Hank threw himself over GW, his shell protecting the old friends from the petrified debris, while Billiam looked up in stunned confusion, his quaking legs frozen to the spot as fragments rained down around him, crushing the last of the surrounding vermin.

Old Brown loomed above, through smoke and debris. He shook his head, knocking free the rodents that gnawed on his ears and sending them spinning into the flames. He grabbed the sides of the hole he'd torn in the great room and flexed, cracking the Rubbish Heap wide like a ribcage. Frances helped Cal to his feet. Together they found GW and Hank and made for the newly made exit, Billiam already way ahead of them.

Once outside, they collapsed to the grass, gulping down fresh air and wiping soot from their skin and fur.

Old Brown punched his fist back into the great room, knocking out another of the supports, causing a large swath of tunnels to collapse like dominoes.

"Is everyone out?" Old Brown asked, glancing back over his shoulder.

Cal performed a quick count and barked, confirming that the party was free from the smoldering wreckage.

Old Brown turned his back on the remains of the Rubbish Heap. He stomped down on a fleeing rat, flattening it into the earth as he stalked toward Cal. For a brief moment, Cal was struck with utter terror, exhausted and helpless before the bear, but as Old Brown stepped to Cal, the bear's demeanor changed, the rage of the attack gone, replaced with a melancholic sigh that seemed to age the elder a decade in seconds. Old Brown grabbed a pawful of Cal's shirt and helped him to his feet. Cal, hesitant at first, extended a paw, thanking the bear, but Old Brown dismissed his gratitude.

"There was enough chaos tonight to rouse a bear from deep mid-winter hibernation. Somehow, Buford made it halfway up my mountain dragging a smoldering wagon. For once I don't want to know the cause."

Cal thought of Buford and wondered if he'd found peace. Old Brown must have read Cal's face, and chuckled, said, "I'm sure he's fine—passed out in the meadow or somewhere along the base of the mount. I gave him a scare worse than the fire, and he turned tailland ran the wagon straight into the river."

They stood across from each other for a long moment, Old Brown gazing off into the distance, Cal unsure of what to say.

"I'm sorry, Cal. I wish it had never come to this. I never trusted you given your history, and I see now that I should have." The bear squinted his eyes, looked out at his mount. "A part of me has been envious of you all these years since the school fire. The way you intervened with little concern for yourself in the moment. The way your *presence* mattered. Even if I'd pushed this body to act, I would have been too slow, too far away to make a difference. All that time spent alone. I think I forgot what I was meant to protect."

Cal opened his mouth to speak, but Old Brown cut him off.

"I'm old, Cal. I knew a sickness was upon our land, the way I feel it in my bones when a storm approaches, but I didn't do enough. For too long I've used the eyes and ears of the community—friends, neighbors . . . even, even, Winifred, at times."

Cal's ears perked up. He felt his chest tighten, suddenly light headed as he hung on every one of the bear's words. He felt something just out of reach, something big, something—

"And . . . Winifred . . . did you . . . ?"

Old Brown looked Cal in the eyes, shook his head and looked away again. "She was one of the sharpest among us. If I'd ever considered there was a chance—"

"Stop, please." Cal held up a paw, and covered his face with the other. He lowered himself to his knees, his mouth filling with saliva. He felt sicker than ever, the events too much to process in the moment.

Old Brown looked down at Cal with a reserved dismay. "It's my time to go, now. Stay out of trouble and give my regards to Gil. The old boy has earned it." Old Brown turned and shuffled off into the dark, his back and legs covered in fresh scratches, cuts, and bites.

19

LATER

Cal leaned back in his chair, watching some of the masked Woods folk dance as the band performed a rather melancholic tune. He wore a nice turtleneck sweater Winifred had given him years ago, and a bear mask the pups had collaborated on, dotted with flowers and missing half an ear. Billiam had gone into overdrive in the week since they'd escaped the fire, working to ensure the Moon Festival honored the lost loved ones, and upheld the tradition of celebrating the past year, making for a somber and joyous affair. The former elected official sat with his head laid on a table two over from Cal, passed out and snoring, exhausted from the early morning preparation, his cat mask (also decorated by his son) askew. The hard work showed—between the decorations, the seven-piece band, the unseasonably warm weather, and strong attendance, it was the best festival in Cal's memory. He ran a paw along the seat of the chair beside him, missing his dear wife, and imagined, as in years past, taking her paw and leading her to the floor for one last dance.

Cal had been unable to shake Old Brown's words over the nights that followed the bear's departure. Cal did his best to piece them together the following week, during the run up to the Moon Festival. At Nutbrown's recommendation, he'd spent time talking with the pups about the recent events, to include Franklin spilling on why they'd gone into the Fells (to meet Old Brown) and confirmation that Winifred had been working for the bear—indeed, one of his many "eyes and ears" that kept him informed in his old age. The revelation of her role, and Old Brown's hand in her death, hurt Cal in ways that stunted his emotions as he tried to hide his pain from the pups, the unknowns worst of all, leaving behind deep scars. Anger and hatred flitted through him like a leaf in the wind, briefly dancing about before disappearing among the trees. He'd tried to grab hold, wallow in rage, but his heart wouldn't let him. Gus and Franklin wouldn't let him. In the past week they'd cried together, sang and told stories together while snuggled in front of the hearth. They had skipped school and taken long walks in the Woods—sometimes aimless, other times along their mother's favorite paths. It wasn't all good, but it was better, and that was what they needed in the moment.

The pups smacked his chair as they ran past, Gus sporting his owl, Franklin in a last-minute beaver, startling Cal. He looked up to see them chased by a white dog dressed in silver. Cal clutched the table for support, nearly falling out of his chair. The dog stopped and looked back at Cal. He felt short of breath, his heart thudding against his chest as she approached—but as she neared he was struck with sudden embarrassment, forced to look away with a whimper.

Frances, wearing a silver dress and plain, unfinished dog mask sat down beside him. "You look like you've seen a ghost."

"I see her everywhere these days."

"How are you, Cal?"

She placed her paw over his on the table, making him fidget for a moment before taking a deep breath to calm his nerves.

"Hanging in there. The pups keep me afloat."

Frances's eyes smiled behind the mask.

"Good to take a load off for a few—those boys possess the energy of a pair of rabbits."

"They're tough to keep up with, that's for sure." Cal pointed out Billiam and they had a nice chuckle, breaking some of the tension.

"He's probably relieved this is his last one."

"I bet he'll be back, offering Helen his services come next year."

Earlier in the day the Woods folk held an impromptu vote to elect a new official. After several animals were nominated and given a moment to speak, the vote was held and tallied, a surprise victory delivered to Helen, the bravest of pigs, over Arnold. The defeated deer had left in a huff while the others celebrated. However, he made his grand entrance to the Moon Festival in good spirits, wearing a pig mask in a display of good gamesmanship.

"Everyone seems to be having a nice time," Frances said, looking out over the crowd. "Did you see GW's new arm?"

Cal nodded. The children had spent an entire school day working on crafting him a new arm out of all available materials, resulting in a rainbow-colored appendage toned with clay, and that had sticks for fingers (six in all). It was attached with a sling over his shoulder, and, to Cal's surprise, fit rather snugly.

"He's being a good sport."

"I think he's rather enjoying it."

Three small children, two rabbits and an otter, the latter holding onto the new limb, danced with GW in a circle as a cluster of children looked on, waiting their turn. Hank and Myrtle danced nearby, the tortoise having not let his friend out of his sight since the night he'd lost his arm.

"Would you care to dance?"

Cal turned back to Frances and observed the rough edges of the mask, how her eyes sparkled behind it in comparison. The similarities to all those years ago so striking it took his breath away.

"Yes."

Cal let her lead him to the dance floor, their friends and neighbors surrounding them, cheering their arrival. The pups cut through the floor, each giving him a smack on the rear as the band started up a slow number and the couples began to dance. Cal took Frances's paw, her dress shimmering in the moonlight. When their eyes met, the magic had gone, leaving Frances behind the mask, but when she smiled he caught a glimpse of it. In the laughter of his sons as they chased each other around the floor. In the scent of the night air. In the beauty of the moon.

ACKNOWLEDGEMENTS

Amid the ongoing pandemic, I feel incredibly fortunate to have had *Ragged* find a home with Titan. Thank you to George Sandison and Lydia Gittins for being wonderful people and welcoming me to the Titan family.

Thank you to Conor Nolan for bringing the world of *Ragged* to life with his incredible illustrations and enthusiastic vision.

Thank you to Katie Eelman for her dedication, friendship, and giving me the push to drop everything and give *Ragged* a shot.

Matthew Revert gave me my first glimpse of Cal fishing along the river. Thank you!

To Paul Tremblay, Jason Ciaramella, Dana Cameron, John Mantooth, Nik Korpon, Angel Colón, Bracken MacLeod, and Errick Nunnally - thank you for the texts, games, calls, and good times from afar that kept the creative mojo alive over the past year.

And to my wife, Jenni, and our boys, George & Fred - on to our next adventure!

ABOUT THE AUTHOR

Christopher Irvin's debut collection, *Safe Inside the Violence*, was a finalist for the 2016 Anthony Award for Best Anthology or Collection. He is also the author of Federales and Burn Cards. He lives in Boston, MA with his wife and two sons.

For more fantastic fiction, author events,
exclusive excerpts, competitions, limited editions and more

VISIT OUR WEBSITE
titanbooks.com

LIKE US ON FACEBOOK
facebook.com/titanbooks

FOLLOW US ON TWITTER AND INSTAGRAM
@TitanBooks

EMAIL US
readerfeedback@titanemail.com